A
VILLAIN'S
Kiss

To those who are broken and don't need a man to put you back together but would appreciate one to help break your bed.
This is for you, queen.

Warning

This book contains sexually explicit scenes and adult language and may be considered offensive to some readers. This book is intended for adults ONLY. Please store your files wisely, where they cannot be accessed by under-aged readers.

Blurb

Savior or seducer.

I am not sure which one he's playing at.

He is forbidden, after all.

I am married to a rockstar.

Appearances must be upheld.

But what does it mean when your marriage is breaking, and the dark, mysterious savior is offering you things you have never had before?

Do you say yes? Or do you say no?

He owns a sex club.

So the promises he is making might very well hold true.

It's risky to do this with a stranger.

But how much of a stranger is he really?

CHAPTER 1

Suck my cock and shut the fuck up

JAKE

T he sounds she's making fill the room.

Why the fuck does she have to moan so loudly? Is she trying to show me how much she enjoys being on her knees sucking my cock.

Because honestly, I couldn't care less.

"Hmm..." My eyes find the television screens in my office, showcasing the views from the cameras situated everywhere throughout the building.

I've been up here for hours. At first, I was working, and now I'm doing anything but.

Her hand lands on my thigh as she tries pushing my legs wider, and I let her. She continues sucking my cock as my eyes lock on one of the screens, where I find a sultry redhead I would recognize anywhere. She stumbles as she moves toward the door, and I watch as a guy reaches out and redirects her. She waves him off with the brush of her fingers.

Fuck, I bet those fingers would be real nice wrapped around my cock.

I glance down at Miranda, or was it Rebecca? Fuck.

I don't know or care.

She offered, so who the fuck was I to say no to a decent pair of lips.

"You can go," I tell her.

She pulls her mouth from my still mostly flaccid cock—she just isn't doing it for me.

It's not her fault.

It's me.

But she doesn't need to know that.

My taste has changed, and I can't pinpoint why. I glance back at the cameras and see the redhead being walked out through the back alleyway—no one goes out that way. Her steps falter again as the club starts to die down. It's close to closing time, but have you tried kicking out a bunch of drunk dickheads? It's damn near impossible to get some semblance of cooperation.

"I can make it hard again." The woman in front of me stands and pulls her tits free. They're cute little tits, I've got to give her that, but they are simply not enough for me to want to continue.

"Just leave. You know the way out." I flick my hand to the door and turn my chair back to my desk, but this woman does *not* take the hint.

Instead, she saunters over to me, her tits still free, and comes to stand behind me. Her hands wrap around my throat, and she leans over me, her chest now pressed against my neck. "But we haven't had any fun yet," she purrs.

I press the button on my desk. A moment later, the door opens and in stalks Captain, also known as Gino, but only I can call him that. To everyone else, he's Captain. We come from a place of understanding. We both ran from our demons and created a life for ourselves. And here we are.

"Captain will see you out," I say. My bored tone makes me sound like an asshole.

She pushes off my chair and huffs. "Really? Maybe the stories are true. I have heard you own this club to watch others fuck because you suck in bed." I give her no reply, just smile as Captain grabs her arm and leads her out. "Fuck you, Jake," she yells as the door shuts behind her. "You limp-dick motherfucker."

I chuckle at that dig because it was a good one. I mean, she did make me soft, so limp-dick is quite fitting.

Focusing back on the screens, I can no longer see

her anywhere inside, so I flick to the alley camera, and what I witness makes my blood boil. I can't get Captain to check it out, and I usually don't get involved with outside drama, but this? This is not acceptable.

CHAPTER 2
Either angel or devil
ORIANA

Rough hands push me back, then one skates up my thigh while the other grips my ass. Hard.

My head spins.

What is happening?

I have to move.

Why aren't I moving?

Come on, legs... Move.

Managing to open one eye, I finally see him.

Who is he?

Do I know him?

Groggily, something leaves my mouth.

Did I make a sound? I'm not sure.

"What the fuck?"

Whose voice is that? It's strong, and it isn't coming from the person who's touching me. No, that person is grunting.

"I suggest you move along," the man holding me roughly says.

Someone grips me firmly. His hand goes directly to my neck and squeezes. My eyesight becomes blurry to the point where I can barely make out faces.

"Get lost," the man above me says.

The new voice is closer now.

"That ain't gonna happen."

My arms start to move—slowly, methodically, inch by inch—then I shove the man's chest and attempt to push him off me, but he merely laughs at my efforts.

I can't remember how I got here.

Where is here?

What's the last thing I remember?

It takes a moment to gain my bearings before I recall going out with the girls for Simone's birthday drinks. *She's my best friend, but she left with someone, and I...* My thought drifts off for a moment as I force my eyes open and try to keep them that way.

Is that his chin? Well, that's what I see first—it's narrow with scruff.

My mind starts to put things back in place, like a jigsaw puzzle.

This asshole asked me to dance.

I said no.

He walked away.

And yet, how am I here with him?

I try pushing again and again, but he hardly moves with my thrusting hands.

"Last chance," the other voice adds.

The man who's hovering over the top of me starts to laugh. "You have no idea who I am."

"I don't care," the stranger replies.

My eyes flutter as I suck in a deep breath, and just as I'm about to scream, my attacker is off me, and the cold instantly assaults my body. Usually I dislike the cold, but right now, I welcome it with great pleasure and hope the warmth doesn't return.

Somehow, I move my legs and manage to roll over. It's then I realize I'm on the ground and still fully clothed, thankfully. The cement bites into my hands as I try to push myself up with every ounce of energy I can muster. However, I don't get far when I hear a loud grunt followed by someone forcing me over.

That's when I fall, and my head hits the ground and bounces. If I didn't already have fuzzy vision, I do now.

Calloused hands touch me, but they're not the same ones from before.

How do I know that? I have no idea.

With what little strength I have remaining, I try to move, but my body is spent.

Why?

Shit.

I was drugged, wasn't I?

"Name?" the stranger asks.

I'm lifted into strong arms before I can respond, my body bouncing and my head lolling as he walks. He smells of the ocean breeze and something far more sinister. Darker.

When he asks my name again, I have nothing to give him. My mind won't cooperate enough to let words escape my lips. I'm telling myself it's simple, *just say your name*, but it's useless because nothing works.

"Woman, I'm taking you to the hospital," he barks.

Those words have me squirming in his arms. *No, no... That's the last place I want to go.*

"Fuck, woman, stay still!"

Somehow, I manage to croak, "No."

"Okay, no hospital. But you need care. You're bleeding."

The heat radiating from his body is too much, and for some reason, I want the cold to return. He starts moving again, this time a little faster.

The heat vanishes as I'm placed on leather, then a car door is closed.

"Sleep," he orders.

I'm not sure why, but in some strange way, right now, I feel safe. Which is ludicrous, considering I have no idea where I am, who I'm with, or what the hell is going on.

Perhaps I'm crazy? I'm not sure.

But I listen to his words and drift off into the blackness.

CHAPTER 3

Is he a god, or married?

ORIANA

"Y ou're finally awake. You've been sleeping all day."

I'm sitting up in a bed I do *not* recognize, in a place I have never been before.

What on earth is this place?

There are beds and couches everywhere, but it's void of people except *him.* My eyes find him sitting on one of the couches, with one leg resting over the other while his hand taps his thigh.

"Where..." *Ah, my voice is back.* It seems everything is back because I feel like I can string a sentence together, and that's what I do when I ask him, "Where am I?"

"In my establishment."

Three words? That's all I get in return.

He's holding a cigar in one hand, the other is still tapping on his leg, though the action looks strained. Tense.

"Why am I here?" I attempt to stand, but my head spins and I instantly see stars, so I sit straight back down.

"Because I caught you in a *situation* last night. One you may not have consented to."

I take him in as he watches me calmly. His dark hair is on the longer side, not overly long but enough so he could tie it back. His eyes, which are almost charcoal in color, seem somewhat intimidating—it's as if they can see right through me. He's tall, dressed in dark jeans, a white button-up shirt, and brown boots.

"And you believe in consent?" I ask. Though after what he did for me, I think the answer is clear.

He waves a single hand around his establishment. "You're in a place where consent is key."

"I'm..." I shake my head, "confused."

"How is your head feeling? The doctor had to add a stitch or two, so you may have a few of those red locks missing."

I immediately reach up and touch the back of my head, where, indeed, some of my hair is missing. "Thank you. What do I owe you?" I ask.

"I have a doctor on hand." He butts out his cigar

and stands. "You were drugged and you've been sleeping it off. In case you weren't coherent enough, he didn't rape you, though he was going to."

"Drugged?" I question, my stomach sinking. "I have to go." I stand, albeit shakily my head going a million miles per hour. Not even thinking of the possibility of what could have happened. As my bare feet touch the floor, I look around for my shoes. "Where are my shoes?"

"I checked around last night but couldn't find them."

When I glance up at him again, he's dangling a pair of exorbitantly expensive pink shoes from his fingers—they're the kind with the bright red soles.

As I step closer, I'm dwarfed by his height. "Those aren't mine."

"I'm aware. Take them."

"What? You just want to give them to me? They're expensive shoes," I say, my brows furrowing.

"Yes. As I said, you've been asleep for a while, and I would like you to leave so I can open my establishment."

I reach out for the shoes, then slide them onto my feet while he stands in front of me.

"What is this place?"

"My establishment," he says again.

"You've said that, but what type of establishment?"

"It has many names. I'm not one for labels." His words make me stop and look back at him.

"What are the *many names*?"

His jaw tightens as if he's agitated with me. But I don't move.

"A sex club, a spotlight party, a whorehouse..." He throws out all three in quick succession, and all I can do is stare at him incredulously.

"Was I just lying on..." My head spins back to the bed, and my forehead crinkles in disgust.

His breath is on my face when he speaks, "Yes, pretty lady, you were lying on a bed where others have fucked. Does it make you feel dirty?"

"I've never been to a whorehouse!"

"Well, now you have."

When I face him again, he starts walking away. I'm not sure how to get out of here, so I follow behind him with my new heels clicking on the beautiful marble flooring until we reach a staircase.

He halts, charcoal eyes finding mine, and he nods to the stairs. "Leave." His voice is firm, and I get the hint.

I take the first step of the stairs, then turn around. "Thank you for helping me. Are you sure I don't owe you anything?"

He doesn't want me here, of that I have no doubt, but I need confirmation. His actions seems too generous, or maybe too kind, for a man like him. Not that I know him, but with this type of establishment and that type of man, there is no doubt he would be a villain.

As silence fills our proximity, my gaze drifts to my red-painted fingernails, chipped and gripping the handrail, then to my knees, which are scratched and stiff, and my dress, that's torn slightly and marred with stains. But it could have been so much worse if not for him.

When I peer back up, his eyes are still glued to mine.

I wait another beat for him to answer, but he doesn't.

So, holding on tightly to the rail, I tread the rest of the steps carefully, trying to keep my balance in my weakened state until I reach the top. The door's shut, and when I pull it open, I look back once more.

"Goodbye, Mrs. Lavender."

Shock must register on my face because he offers me a small smirk before I continue out the door.

I step into an alleyway, and suddenly relief hits me hard.

If anyone, including my husband, saw me leaving a sex club, it would be all over the papers and television.

He would *not* be impressed.

Imagine the uproar if the paparazzi got hold of this.

We have the perfect tabloid image, and I could have ruined it in one fell swoop.

CHAPTER 4

My husband is an ass

ORIANA

My hand goes to my hair, and I subconsciously start twirling it as I stand on our perfectly manicured green grass and look up at our big, beautiful house. It's in a secluded, gated community so the general public cannot enter. It's all a part of having money, and Kyler, my husband, has a lot of it. I lick my lips and wonder what I will say to him. How do I tell my husband about the situation I found myself in, or even begin to explain what happened when even I am unsure?

I was one of the lucky ones, it seems.

But still, it's left me shaken, and I am forever thankful to *that man* who owns the club.

The door opens, and there he stands, my husband, dressed in a casual tee that has an incredibly expensive logo written all over it and a pair of designer jeans. The whole outfit probably costs more than a damn small car. It's insane.

I wonder when we changed.

How we changed.

Why we changed.

Kyler smiles at me, and my heart doesn't miss a beat like it should. Instead, it fills with dread. Dread over how I know I have to walk up to that door, holding on to an expensive pair of shoes that another man gave me, and tell him what happened.

Do I tell him?

He'll find out one way or another.

Maybe he won't.

I like the second possibility better.

Taking a deep breath, I move my bare feet through the grass until they hit the perfectly paved entrance to the front of the house. Kyler holds the door open for me while still smiling.

That smile used to make me drop to my knees, worshipping the man in front of me.

I loved him with all I am.

I married young—we were high school sweethearts.

He was my...everything.

Kyler and I thought we would be together forever. Not once did I imagine us drifting apart and becoming two strangers who simply share a house. But somehow, this is exactly what we've become. People grow apart, it's a fact of life, but for some reason, I never thought it would happen to us.

Kyler looks me up and down. "Good, you're home. I'm off." He leans in and kisses my cheek, then looks down at the shoes in my hand and dress. "New dress? I like it," he comments before he strides out of the house without a "Why are you late?" or "Where have you been all night?" Not even a "How was your girls' night?"

Somehow, when the fame increased, I heard a lot of *"Don't you do anything to embarrass me,"* and then it became, *"it's best you stay home."*

And I did.

There was a lot of staying home.

Too much.

So much that I lost who I was in our relationship and became everything he needed.

I need to break from that way of thinking.

It isn't healthy, I know this, but for some unknown reason, I never left.

How do I give up on someone I have given ten years of myself to?

I'm getting close to my thirties, and my needs and wants are not the same as they once were.

What do I even want? The answer to that question is lost on me too.

Now I handle all things, my husband. He has a manager, sure, but I am practically his assistant and schedule everything for him. Like right now, as he gets into his Porsche, I know he is off to record his next album, and he'll be there all night. He works better at night.

Kyler is talented, crazily so. He's stepped away from playing music to writing and producing for other artists. He's had hits all over the world, and his songs have been sung by the biggest names.

He is important.

Whereas I am... Well, I'm nothing more than just me.

I'm not even sure when I let that happen, maybe it's because we were married so early I just gave him my all and got lost along the way. And in doing so I lost my own identity.

Who am I important to? I would hope to my husband, but I'm not so sure anymore. Everything between us feels transactional.

The last time he kissed me like he missed me was over a year ago. And even then, it was put on for the cameras.

That's his number one rule. Don't do anything that could embarrass him especially in front of the cameras.

So I don't.

I am hardly ever seen out and spend most of my time locked in this house doing work for him.

I glance down at the white marble floor. I picked it out. Actually, I picked gray, and Kyler overrode me with white, but the stone and shape were all me. The walls are stark white, and the furniture is much the same, with the occasional gray accent. It almost looks like a hospital in here. The only place you can tell is used is my office.

Kyler hired a cleaner to come twice a week, as he wants everything spotless.

Mess doesn't bother me, it never has.

I walk over and push a cushion purposely off the couch to give the area a semi lived-in feel. Then I walk up the stairs, gripping the glass railing, and go straight to my bedroom. It's *our* bedroom, but nothing sexual happens in here anymore. I can't remember the last time he fucked me. And sometimes a wife just wants to be fucked. Slammed up against the wall and have her husband ravish her.

The last time we had sex, it felt like a chore.

The sad part? I still love him, and I think he's attractive. He came third on the best-looking list in *People* magazine's "The Sexiest Man Alive" issue. Everyone tells me how lucky I am to have him, while I whisper to myself how lucky he is to have me. I signed up for this life—I know I did—but knowing I made this choice doesn't make it any easier.

Stripping out of the dress, I watch as it falls to the floor. I plan for it to be burned so I never see it again.

Then I remember the grunting, and my body locks tight, freezing in place.

What did the man who saved me do to the other man? I should have asked. Maybe I'll go back and ask.

I shake my head. *No, no, I don't want to know.*

But what if there are photos? I cringe at the thought of evidence from what happened spreading around.

And then I tell myself not to be stupid, and it wasn't my fault.

The hot water from the shower steams up the mirror as I look at myself. My red hair is a mess of curly locks in need of a good brush, and my green eyes are sleepy and scared.

How could Kyler walk past me and not see there was something wrong?

I turn away from my hazy reflection, then step into the shower and wet my head. The minute I do, I pull back and cover my mouth as a scream rips out of me so loud I scare myself. My body shakes with the pent-up exhaustion and after-effects of whatever drug that asshole gave me.

Then I remember *stitches.*

Deciding against washing my hair, I scrub the rest

of my body before I step out, grab a fluffy white towel, and wrap myself in it.

Today I had plans. There are many work chores to organize.

But as I look at my bed, I know I can't function, so I climb in, acknowledging I'll be doing absolutely nothing.

I grab my phone and try to search for the man who helped me, but I have no clue what the place is called or even how to look for him. I remember the location, and that's it.

Maybe I will go back.

Or maybe I should let sleeping dogs lie and never visit that place again.

The last option is definitely the safest.

CHAPTER 5

Am I biddable?

"**A**re you ready?"

I slide on my heels as Kyler walks in, dressed in a suit with a bright blue tie to match his light blue shirt. I spent all week in bed, and not once did my husband ask what was wrong with me or if I was okay. Come to think of it, I hardly saw him until he kindly reminded me yesterday of the gala we are to attend tonight.

I considered telling him no.

I wanted to tell him no.

But I knew it was time to stop ordering food, laying in bed all day and night, and I was going to have to start living again.

I didn't automatically fall in love with Kyler in high school. In fact, he was dating someone else the first time we spoke. We ended up having English together and were paired up for an assignment. I had known who he was, but we had never really spoken. I wasn't in the same circles he was in. Not that I didn't have friends, I simply didn't have as many friends as he did. Kyler was born to be famous. He's the kind of person everyone loves.

I came to realize early on I understood why.

He had charm.

Charisma.

The man was captivating.

I could sit there and listen to him talk for hours.

By the end of our senior year, he was single, and he casually asked me to go to a party. At the time, I thought I may not have heard him right because Kyler, the most popular guy in our school, wanted to take me, a lover of everything he isn't, to a party.

He played his guitar on breaks at school.

I sat in a corner and read books.

I wanted to be a doctor and was studying to achieve that goal, but then I fell for Kyler, and from that day, I agreed to almost everything he asked.

Even the stupid things.

He was my first, well, everything.

When he said he wanted to move to a different state after graduation to pursue his musical aspirations, I told him I would follow. When he asked me for help managing his books and personal affairs, I gladly accepted.

In return, I lost me.

My identity.

My soul and essence.

"Are those your new heels?" Kyler asks, motioning to my shoes from the doorway. I am wearing a silver dress, with heels that don't belong to me. But I guess they do now. I glance down at them and remember the man with charcoal eyes, then look back to my husband's hazel eyes and nod my head.

"Hmm..." he replies before he turns and walks off.

I grind my molars before taking one last look at myself in the mirror. My silver dress is long and has a small train at the back. With a split up the side, it hugs my body and shows a fair amount of cleavage. No straps hold it in place, but it is tied at the back. I fought with the idea of adding a necklace, but in the end, I decided less is more with this color. I grab a pink purse to match my pink shoes and walk outside to find my husband already sitting in the car, waiting. I slide in next to him, and the driver takes off.

"How has your week been?" I ask more out of making conversation than actually caring about what he's been doing.

Kyler doesn't turn to look at me anymore, and when he answers, his eyes are glued to his phone.

"Busy. I see you managed to get out of bed today," he replies. There isn't malice in his voice, but there's no concern either.

"I did. I was feeling a little off this week."

"I hope you're over whatever it was. I need you back full force next week."

He wasn't always like this.

Or maybe he was?

Love lets your mind play tricks on you.

My love for Kyler allowed me to let him rule me. Without even realizing he was doing so. He wasn't controlling or manipulative, he was just…

Kyler demanded, and I gave in, always finding it hard to say no to him.

I still do.

"You look nice," I tell him.

His fingers pause on his phone, and he glances over at me. His attention went straight to my chest. "Can you pull your dress up? Paparazzi are about to take photos, and I would rather them not take any of your tits." I look down at my strapless dress and see it's fallen down a fraction. I wiggle it back up and sigh.

My tits are fake.

Why are they fake? My husband thought one day it would be better if I had bigger boobs.

I agreed, so bigger boobs are what I got.

Now I hate them.

Biting my tongue, I look out the window as the car speeds along.

How is it possible to still love someone but not want to be with them? Because I do very much love my husband, but I think sometimes I would be better off without him.

Doing what? I don't even know.

The car comes to a stop, and the driver gets out and opens my door.

"Your top. Hold it up," Kyler reminds me as I reach for the driver's hand to slide out onto my feet. I do as Kyler says, holding my dress firmly, and step out. Cameras start flashing, and I put on my best smile as I turn to look back at my husband as he exits the car.

We have been called the "it" couple.

Unbreakable.

Kyler's hand rests on the small of my back as he waves his other hand at the cameras and guides me forward. I go willingly and smile for the cameras as we make our way along the red carpet and up the stairs to the entrance of the gala. It's full of influential people, governors, police chiefs, lawyers, and those who scream money and power. We've been coming to these things for years. To be honest, I'm over them. Maybe I'm having an early mid-life crisis? Is that a thing?

It has to be because when I glance at my husband

next to me, I think, *who would ever willingly leave this man?*

He is beautiful in every sense of the word.

So the question is? When he touches me now, why do I want to pull away?

Is it because we have both slowly drifted apart over time?

Maybe he pulled away first, and I just didn't realize it.

The doors close behind us, and I suck in a breath. There aren't any cameras in here, so Kyler's hand drops from my back immediately. He smiles at someone and turns to me.

"A scotch on ice." He gives me his drink order before he walks off.

I look around at all the eyes following him. He carries himself in such a way people can't help but stare.

Sighing, I go to the bar and lean on it as I pull my phone from my bag. I flick through messages I haven't answered for days. There are some from my parents, asking when they can visit next. My brother, who just sends me question marks now. And then there are a few from my best friend, who left me that night at the bar before I was drugged.

"Oriana." *Speak of the devil.* I turn at my name being called by my best friend, sliding my phone in my purse as I smile at her. "I thought that was you. You haven't replied to me, and I was getting worried." Her long blonde hair falls down her back in neat curls. She's wearing a black dress that is a little too tight, but she pulls it off amazingly.

"I've been busy," I tell her as the bartender steps over. "A margarita and a scotch on the rocks, please," I tell the bartender.

"You changed your drink," Simone comments next to me. I met Simone through Kyler. She was an agent who was trying to pitch Kyler, but he already had an agent, and we became fast friends instead.

"Yes, figured it was time for a change." What I usually drink would only remind me of *that night*, and that's the last thing I want to think about.

"Did you have a good time on our girls' night? I had so much fun and the man who I went home with... Well, let me tell you...he was amazing in bed. Like, hold the sheets amazing."

"Hmm," is the only response I care to give.

"He called me yesterday. He wants to meet up again."

"That's nice."

The bartender brings my drinks, and I lift mine to my lips. The salt hits me first, and I take a sip. My eyes go wide at the taste of the tequila. *Wow, now that is a drink.*

"Have you never had a margarita before?" she jokes.

I haven't. I had one drink I liked, and I stuck to it. Maybe that's what I'm good at? Sticking with things, even when they no longer suit me.

"I gotta get back to Kyler. Chat later?" I ask her.

Simone lays her hand on my arm as I lift both drinks. "Are you mad at me? You seem—"

"I'm fine, just tired. I had a busy week." She nods at my words before I walk away.

I find my husband talking to a bunch of men I don't recognize. Then again, I hardly recognize anyone he speaks to. I tend to zone out and politely nod my head at things he says at functions like this, hoping I am nodding at the right times. Sliding up behind him, I squeeze in and hand him his drink. He takes it without thanking me, and I stand there quietly.

"This must be Oriana." I smile at the voice as Kyler looks down at me.

"It is. Oriana, meet Sergio."

I smile at the new chief of police.

"I've heard nothing but good things about you." He takes my hand and kisses it.

My smile remains in place as I pull my hand back. "It's a pleasure to meet you," I reply.

"I'm looking forward to bidding on you tonight," Sergio says, and I glance up at him, confused.

Kyler places an arm around my waist. "Oriana doesn't know yet. I was going to leave it as a surprise, but you just gave it away, Chief." I catch my husband's hazel eyes as he peers down at me. "You know how you wanted to raise money for the children's cancer foundation?" I nod in acknowledgment. "They asked for an item to bid on, and I suggested a date with you."

"A date?" I gasp.

Kyler squeezes my side as I gape at him, shocked.

"I'll be sure to win it, Oriana. Maybe we can go out on patrol together. I'll show you what a real man does."

Kyler laughs as he excuses us and leads us away.

When we are out of earshot, I turn to face him. "Have you lost your mind?" I seethe as I push away from him, and he glances around to make sure no one can hear us.

"Figured you may like this." He shrugs. "And keep your voice down. Someone may hear you."

An announcement comes over the speakers, and I lock eyes with the man I love. *Loved?* Which is it? I don't even know anymore.

"I'm not a prize to be bid on, Kyler."

"Would you rather not help the children?" he throws back at me.

That's not fair, and he knows it. My sister passed away from bone cancer when I was only ten. I hate that he did this, knowing full well I can't back down from it because it would be a slap in the face for my deceased sister.

I hear my name called, and Kyler leans in and kisses my cheek. "I would never let any other man win you. It's me who will be winning the bid."

I breathe a sigh of relief as he walks off, and I follow after him as my name is called again. Making my way to the stage, I stand next to the hostess as everyone is seated. I spot my husband in the front row with a drink in his hand as he talks to the chief of police next to him.

"The bidding will begin at fifty-thousand dollars." I swing my head around at the sound of the hostess's voice who I wasn't even listening to, to begin with.

Sergio calls out, "Sixty thousand." I look at my husband next to him, waiting for him to bid and he does.

"Sixty-five." He winks at me as the hostess asks for another bid.

I sigh and smile.

It goes quiet until Sergio speaks up again, "Seventy."

My gaze lands on my husband, and he smiles and says, "Seventy-five." I manage to keep a smile on my face.

"Any last bids?"

Everything goes quiet, and everyone in the room is deathly silent before I hear someone loudly say, "Half a million dollars."

My eyes search for *that voice*, and when I find the owner, I lock eyes with the man whose charcoal eyes have been haunting my dreams. He offers me a smirk and tips his head. When I look at my husband again, he just shakes his head, telling me he will no longer bid.

Shit.

Shit.

I guess I'm going on a date with a man who isn't my husband.

Well fuck.

CHAPTER 6

Mrs. to you

A s she steps off the stage, I follow her with my gaze. Her husband walks straight up to her and puts an arm around her waist as she leans in and whispers something in his ear.

"You sure you should have done that, boss?" Captain asks from his seat next to me.

I pick up my glass and smile over the top of it. "Probably not, but it was fun."

"You do love to bid and win."

I do.

It's how I run many of my businesses—the ones that make the most money, that is.

"Heads up... Here they come," Captain says.

I stand as she and Kyler approach, taking her in as she does the same to me. Her gaze scans over me, looking up and down before stopping at my eyes.

"This was a surprise. I didn't think you could make it tonight," Kyler says.

"I did have an invite, and it's for a good cause, right?" He nods and turns to his wife, who hasn't taken those gorgeous green eyes off me.

"You know my husband?" she asks me. I smirk, not being able to help myself. The real question should have been how her husband knows me.

"I do," I answer her.

"How?" she asks as she turns her head toward her husband.

"Oriana," Kyler says, trying to hide his annoyance at her curiosity. "Jake is a major donor to a lot of charities. He makes incredibly large donations to worthwhile charities."

"Does he?" she asks, looking back at me with a lifted brow. "And can I ask what it is you do for a living..." She pauses. "Jake, was it?"

"Yes, and you're Oriana." I offer her my hand, and she hesitates at first. I fight the smirk that wants to pull at my lips as she glances at her husband and then at my hand. When she finally holds her hand out, I take it. It's small and delicate in mine. I notice her once-red nails are now silver to match her dress. Turning her hand over, I lean in and kiss her inner wrist softly before I meet her eyes again.

Oriana pulls her hand from mine and slides it

behind her back. I see a blush take hold of her cheeks, while I am watching her with great interest.

"Jake owns a lot of things. I'd say his clubs are his biggest money-makers. Isn't that right, Jake?" Kyler continues.

"Clubs? What type of clubs?" Oriana pushes.

"Dance clubs, Oriana. What has gotten into you?"

She scrunches her nose up before she looks back at me.

"Among other things," I offer her. Those green eyes that remind me of a rainforest pierce me.

"Seems you get the pleasure of taking my wife out. I know you will be a gentleman and keep your hands to yourself, of course," Kyler says. But he doesn't mean it. He says it because he thinks he has to. I stand by as Oriana grabs his arm and leans on him.

"A gentleman." I laugh and look at Oriana. "Is that what you would prefer me to be for the night?"

Captain coughs behind me, and I don't move an inch as her cheeks turn from pink to red. Kyler doesn't say anything. Either he trusts his wife, or he doesn't care. I think it's probably the latter.

"Yes, of course," she says meekly.

"Good. I'll collect you on Sunday." I turn to Captain, who is pretending not to pay any attention, and nod toward the door.

"Sunday?" She gasps.

Facing her again, I refrain from smirking. I like seeing her sweat. The way her cheeks match the color of her hair makes me wonder if it matches other things...

"Do you have an issue with that?" I ask.

"No, she's free." Kyler nods and turns to leave. "Have a good night, Jake."

As soon as Kyler is gone, she steps closer to me.

"Is your name really Jake?"

"Does the red of the drapes match the carpet?" I ask her. She swallows hard at my vulgar question, and Captain simply chuckles behind me.

"How dare you ask a married woman that."

"Where is your ring?" I ask, noticing she's not wearing one.

Those green eyes flick down, and she instantly shakes her head. "I forgot. I had a busy week."

"I'm sure you did."

"What is that meant to mean?" She scoffs. "Are you saying I'm lying?"

I step closer to her and lean into her ear. "I'll see you Sunday, Oriana."

"That's Mrs. Lavender to you." She spins on her heel, and as she does, her red hair flicks my face. I watch as she stalks off, her ass moving hypnotizingly in that tight as fuck silver dress.

"You are playing with fire," Captain says.

"Fire is meant to burn," I reply with a sly grin.

CHAPTER 7
Fool me once...
ORIANA

The audacity of that man, coming here and bidding on me, then proceeding to kiss my wrist in front of my husband.

Who does he think he is?

Dressed in an all-black suit with a black tie, hair messy but somehow perfect—he's a conundrum. An enigma.

Then there are those charcoal eyes that don't just undress you, they penetrate you.

"We need one more item," I hear the hostess say to Kyler as I approach. She is leaning in rather close to him, and it tightens my chest.

"One more?" I ask her, confused.

She spins and puts on a fake smile for me. "Yes, to meet our goal, we need one more item."

"I have the perfect thing. Do you mind?" I take the

microphone from her and, before my husband can say anything or try to stop me, I walk on stage and give the crowd a big smile. I lock eyes with the man sitting at the back table and wonder if he can see the glint in mine.

"Ladies and gentlemen, before we bid you good-night, we have one last item up for grabs." A few people start to clap, but I don't take my eyes off Jake. "He is a business owner, single, has eyes that can strip you bare, and we all know he's a mystery."

At first, everyone is silent. I keep my eyes pinned on him as his jaw clenches. "Jake, if you wouldn't mind coming to the stage. The ladies need to see what they are paying for." He stays where he is as people clap their encouragement.

I offer him my best *fuck-you* smile as he stands and makes his way to the stage. I track him with my gaze as he strides over to me, not once looking at the audience in front of us. When Jake reaches me, he leans in and places a hand on the small of my back. Goose bumps cascade all over my skin, and I suck in a breath when he whispers, "I'm not the man you want to play games with."

I whisper back, "Games? Whatever do you mean? Charity is all we are here for." I turn to leave as the hostess walks up and takes the microphone to start bidding.

"Stay," he commands quietly.

I lick my lips and get one step away before he speaks again, "Stay, or I'll tell your husband the way you are looking at me is not the way a married woman should look at another man."

I pause as the hostess starts the bidding. As I turn to face him, he doesn't even care that everyone in this room is focusing on us as he stares at me. "Now, bid."

"I..."

"I know you have money, Oriana. So bid." The way he says my name makes everything in me go on high alert. He shouldn't have that much power.

I scan the crowd for my husband. He isn't even paying attention as he leans against the bar, talking to yet another woman.

Does he cheat on me? I hope not, but I can't be sure.

I have never cheated. And this dance Jake and I are doing right now feels wrong. Like I am tempting fate. But I can't seem to move away, no matter how hard I try.

"No," I bite back.

Without turning his head away from me, he eyes the crowd as an older woman calls out her bid, and then another woman. They have no shame in bidding on him, and I see the appeal, I really do.

"Would you like me to tell you a secret about your husband?"

"We don't have secrets."

He laughs, again showing no concern that a crowd of people are watching our exchange. Jake leans down, hovering over me, and all I can smell is the ocean. I have decided I now hate the smell of the ocean.

"So you wouldn't like to know which club of mine he has visited?" he asks, his gaze intense.

My breathing stops and I shake my head.

"Bid."

"One hundred thousand," I call out.

He tsks at my offer.

An older lady in the room cackles and bids higher.

"You can do better," he whispers.

"Three hundred thousand," I say, then look back at him. "That's my last one. I don't have anymore."

Someone offers half a million, and Jake gives me an expectant look.

"I can't," I insist.

"Bid. *Now.*"

"No," I say, crossing my arms over my chest.

His eyes fall to my breasts, and he licks his lips before he shakes his head.

"One million," he says and then points to me. "You will give me two dates." He glances over to the hostess and orders, "End it," before he stalks off, leaving me standing there, baffled.

Did he just bid on himself for me?

Walking off the stage, I find Kyler waiting for me.

"Seems you have caught the eye of Jake," he says as if all that didn't just happen right in front of his eyes.

"Do you still love me?" I ask.

Kyler studies me, and that's all it takes for me to know.

Looking into his eyes, I don't see the man who once loved me as if I am his everything. I see a man who sees me as a burden, just something to keep his name clean. "Actually, don't answer that. I already know the answer... It's just taken me a while to get there." I turn to walk away, but he grabs my arm.

"We'll talk when we get home," he says.

That's when he should have told me I was being silly and that he does love me. But no, those words don't leave his mouth.

And his silence alone breaks my heart a little more.

I pull my arm free and walk out straight to the waiting car.

And I go home.

Alone.

———

KYLER DOESN'T SHOW up until I'm fast asleep that night. And even if I'd been awake, by then, I didn't have the energy to talk to him.

When I wake the next morning, I turn over to see him lying on his stomach, still sleeping. I grab my phone and flick it open while I wait for him to rouse.

Unknown: I prefer my ladies in red.
Dress in red.

I STARE AT THE MESSAGE, confused. I go to delete it, and then I realize who it's from.

Me: I prefer my men dressed in
pink. Dress in pink.

"YOU'RE AWAKE." I turn to see Kyler with one eye open, his face smooshed into his pillow as he looks at me.

"Yes. Seems you didn't come home at a decent enough time to talk. Does us as a couple even matter to you anymore?" I get straight to it because I no longer care.

He groans and turns onto his back. "Of course you matter."

"So, do you love me?" As I say it, I hear how desperate it sounds. I shouldn't be asking my husband these questions. I should know, without a doubt, he does.

"You know I do," he replies.

"You may love me, Kyler, but are you still *in love* with me?"

"What does that even mean?" he asks, shaking his head and getting up from the bed like I'm bothering him. Like my questions mean nothing. My eyes are locked on him as he stands, he reaches for his basket-ball shorts, slides them on, and walks to the door.

"It means you stay and talk instead of running off like a bitch."

His hand grips the doorknob as he sucks in a breath and turns around to face me. "Where has this attitude come from?" My frustration rises as his head leans to the side. It's condescending before he even speaks, "Have I not been showing you enough affection?"

"I'm not a dog, Kyler," I bite back. My phone dings and I pay it no mind.

"I never once said you were."

"Just answer me," I beg, and I hate myself for it.

"I can't," he says simply, and I feel something deep inside of me shatter and break. I mean, I've always known the truth but never had to face it until now. We were so great for so many years. Or maybe that was merely what I wanted to think, and behind it all was some sort of façade.

"I'm going to make this easier on both of us." I stand from the bed. "I'll move out, find a place not far from here, find someone to replace me, and go from there."

"I don't want you to leave," Kyler says, his tone growing urgent. But I know it's not because he's afraid of losing my love.

"So what do you want?" I ask. He scratches the back of his head, and I watch his arm muscles flex. "See, you can't even answer that." I shake my head. "I've been trying, Kyler. You and me? I thought we would last forever. Through fame and everything else, we stuck it out, yet here we are...in this situation." I grind my teeth when he shows me no emotion. "You can't seem to do it, so I guess I'll have to be the one to handle this." Walking to the closet, I grab a suitcase and throw it open and start packing.

"What about my meetings?" My hand freezes, and I spin on my knees to see him staring at me. *He's unbelievable.*

"That's what you're worried about as your wife sits

in our closet packing her things? You're worried about your meetings?" I ask incredulously.

"Well, no...and yes." I grunt and turn back to continue packing. "I don't want you to leave, Oriana, but I'm not going to stop you either."

"I want a *man* to stop me, Kyler. I want a *man* who is crazy for me. Someone for whom the thought of me leaving him sends him into a blinding rage. You just aren't that man, are you?" Glancing back at him, I see him looking down at his phone. I grab the nearest shoe and hurl it at him. "You see that shoe right there? I got that at one of Jake's clubs when I was almost raped, you prick. He saved me, got me a doctor, and all the while, you didn't even know I didn't come home. Or should I say you didn't care."

"Jake?" he asks, surprised. "You went to a sex club?" He stares at me with a dazed look of bewilderment which tells me everything I need to know.

"No, you fool. I was at a dance club." I throw my other shoe at him. "Get out. Just get out and let me pack."

"I want it noted that I didn't want this," he states, then goes to open the door again.

"Have you fucked anyone else but me since we've been together?" I ask before he leaves.

Kyler lifts his eyes from his phone and locks them on me. "No," he answers.

A sigh leaves me.

"Though I have thought about it."

I feel the tear leave my eye instantly. I can't stop it, and I quickly swipe it away. "I'll find a lawyer to draw everything up," I tell him.

"I won't give you any of my business, Oriana. I worked too damn hard for it." I take a deep breath and remember not to kill my husband. I say nothing and keep on packing. "I mean it," he adds. "Everything here is mine. You can take your things, but that's it." I throw another shoe at him, hitting the doorway instead of my target as he finally walks out. He wouldn't be where he is if it wasn't for me. I helped him get there, and I helped him maintain his status.

Fuck him.

I hear his footsteps as he walks away, then listen closely as the front door shuts. My phone starts to ring, and I answer it without even thinking twice.

"Pink?" the voice on the other end questions. I pull the phone away from my ear and note it's a private number.

"Now is not the time." A hiccup leaves me, and I struggle to hold back the tears.

"Are you crying?" Jake's voice floats through the phone.

"Yes, I'm currently packing my stuff and getting '*only my things*' out as requested by my soon-to-be ex-husband. I have to go. I need to work out what I'm going to do." I hang up before he can say another word. I should have asked why he was calling, but the last thing on my mind is what Jake wants.

I have half the closet packed and ready to go when my doorbell rings. While I head downstairs, I make sure to wipe away my tears before I pull the door open.

A man is standing there, dressed in a mover's outfit.

"Oriana?" he asks.

"Yes, that's me," I answer.

"Perfect. Where should we start?" He comes right in, and I look at him, confused.

"Start?"

"Yes, moving your things. We received an urgent request."

"From whom?"

He checks his paperwork before he answers, "Jake."

CHAPTER 8

Take that, bitch

I took everything I purchased.

Everything.

I left the asshole with one couch and his office untouched. Not because I was being vile but because it was all technically mine. He seems to have conveniently forgotten that fact. I wonder if he even realizes it was me who paid all the bills. Yes, he is the major money earner, but I also earn a wage.

This reminds me I'll have to find another job. Thankfully, I have saved a lot of money while we were together. Not thinking a day like this would come, but just because my mother always taught me to save.

I was able to move straight into my brother's place. He lives alone, and he's local, and even better, he is usually away, traveling. He takes photographs for a living, something to do with scenery.

Tonight, he's off to Iceland of all places. It's his favorite place to take his pictures and he is amazing at what he does. He started by taking photos of Kyler, then left him early on to do what he does now. And he hasn't looked back.

I stand back as the mover brings the last box into my brother's kitchen, and I cringe when I see it's all taking up so much room. Luckily for him, he has a three-bedroom home. And while I will have one, all my stuff is about to be crammed into the second bedroom.

"How much do I owe you?" I ask the mover, and he smiles.

"All paid for, plus a big tip." He winks before he leaves. *Paid for?* I reach for my phone and call Jake straight away.

"Thank you," I say quickly before I hang up, not wanting to hear what he has to say because I don't want to have jumbled thoughts right now.

I've only just left my husband, a man who I thought I would be married to forever. I guess his version of forever and mine are two entirely different things.

"Shit, how am I meant to move around in here?" Harvey asks, looking around as he enters the house with his camera slung around his neck.

"I'll move most of it," I tell him. My hands slide to my hips as my phone starts ringing. When I see Kyler's face flash on the screen, I put it down on one of the boxes.

"It will get easier," Harvey says, and I wipe away the tear that managed to escape.

"Are you sure?"

"Day by day, it will get easier."

I take him at his word. Harvey has never lied to me, and he has experienced heartbreak. His college sweetheart died right before he was going to ask her to marry him. That's when he quit work and started traveling.

"He doesn't love me anymore," I say on a sob.

"Do you still love him?" he asks. I raise my brows at him. "Don't shoot me, but have you seen yourself lately? Neither of you looks happy around the other. Like it's a chore. It's been like that for years, O, and I can't even remember the last time I saw you two kiss on the lips instead of his usual kiss on the cheek." I sit on the floor, releasing a heavy breath. "All I'm saying is you gave up so much for that man. It's time to start living for you for a change. Don't fall victim to loving someone so much you change who you are meant to be."

"I don't know who that person is anymore." I turn my tear-filled eyes to him.

"Maybe not today, but you will." He kisses the top of my head and walks to his room, climbing over the boxes as he goes.

My phone rings again, and this time I take a breath and answer it.

"Come back. I wasn't thinking right," Kyler says.

I close my eyes and let my head fall to the box in front of me as I listen to him breathing through the phone. "I can't," I reply on a broken whisper. "I can't."

"You can. Come back. Please. It was a mistake. I don't want anyone but you," he begs.

"You do, though, Kyler, and that's okay. We've changed."

"Oriana."

"Yes?"

"I do love you."

"And I love you, Kyler. Nothing can erase that love. You were my favorite person for more than a decade. But we aren't the same people anymore. I wish you nothing but the best, you know that. But I need to be me and see how me is without you."

"Then you will come back?" he asks.

And I'm taken aback when I answer without hesitation, "No," I say firmly. I wait for him to speak again, but we both stay silent. My tears fall down my cheeks and drip off my chin onto the floor as my head leans on the box. I watch as they form a puddle, and it spreads out.

"What do I do when I'm nervous, Kyler?" I ask and wait a heartbeat for him to answer.

"Pace?" he says, and I can hear the uncertainty in his voice.

"No, wrong answer."

I hang up and wonder if he even knows me at all and if this was always a one-sided relationship.

———

HARVEY LEAVES, and I'm left in his house to work out my life. What type of life do I want? I don't even know who I am outside of Kyler anymore.

And he is not to blame for that.

I am.

I should have seen it from the beginning.

I gave him my all, and he just took, and took, and took.

I spend the rest of the week doing nothing. Boxes remain unpacked, but I managed to move some around, so they are not in the way. A private number keeps calling me, but I know who it is. I'm meant to go out with him tomorrow, but I don't want to. Not because it's him but because of what I might do.

I'm not in the right frame of mind for any of this.

Not in the right frame of mind for a man.

Kyler calls once. I expected at least a few attempts, but I have a feeling the last time he called was because he came home to an empty house and panicked.

A loud knock sounds at the door. I sit up on the couch and look at it. Is Harvey expecting someone? Did he forget to tell someone he went away? I stay where I am, not wanting to answer until the knock comes again.

"Oriana." I groan at the sound of *that* voice.

I hate how I recognize it already.

I hate that it sends shivers all over my body.

"You have food at your door, did you know?"

I sigh and pull myself up from the couch, then make my way to the door. Pulling it open, I come face-to-face with a man who single-handedly made me realize my husband doesn't love me without him doing a single damn thing.

"You look..." he stands there, dressed in black dress pants and a black button-up shirt, holding in his hands my Chinese food I ordered and may have forgotten about, "different."

I give him an eye roll and reach for the food, but he snatches it away.

"Good. Now can you leave again."

"Do you swear?" he asks.

"Swear?"

"Yes. Do you say, fuck, whore, dick, cock?" I feel my cheeks flushing at his words. "You don't. I bet you do in your head, though. I bet you have a solid vocabulary in your head."

How can he even pick up on that? I scrunch my nose up at his words.

"I'm right." His grin is smug.

"You should leave now."

"We have a date."

"It's not Sunday," I remind him.

Jake checks his TAG Heuer watch, and I give him another eye roll.

"It is," he replies.

Shit.

I *do* swear.

Just not out loud.

"You know what, I can see that you are all types of fucked-up." I gape at him and blink a few times. He hands me my food, but he doesn't leave straight away. "I paid the charity donation from the auction. I'll be back in a few months to collect on your debt. I expect those dates, Oriana." He releases my food and turns to walk off. I stand there, baffled.

Did he just?

How rich is he?

I watch him as he leaves, confused by everything that just happened. And wondering why, when I see him get into his car, a small smile touches my lips.

CHAPTER 9
Women are crazy

JAKE

A woman I barely know makes me go fucking crazy. How is that even possible? My work is all about women. I know women. They're what I'm good at. I know how to please a woman, how to talk to a woman, and how to give her what she wants. Yet one single redhead has thrown me off my game.

I've known who Oriana is for a long time. I've had business with Kyler on numerous occasions. But his pretty wife was always busy working, for him. Attached to his arm and too oblivious to realize that other people were looking at her.

I don't make it a thing to go after married women.

In fact, I stay away from them.

I have a club that lets all people—married or single —do whatever it is they want.

I meet women from all over the world.

I even buy women. Yes, that's right. And I will continue to do that.

Maria stands next to me at an auction. In the middle of the room are a bunch of women on a rotating platform. The platform turns, showing all the people around the circle each and every woman they can choose from.

Human trafficking.

It's the hidden underground I hate.

But I play the part and do what I can.

I may be evil, but I was raised by women. I respect women more than anything. So this? This is what I do to protect those I can.

"The bidding price is quite high," Maria comments. Maria is my cousin. Like I said, raised by women.

"Get the blonde." I nod to the small out-of-her-brain one who looks as if she is barely standing. "And the brunette." Who is currently itching her arms as if she can scratch her way out of her skin.

"I don't know if we have enough for two," Maria says.

"Work it out, Maria."

She nods before she picks up the iPad they use to take the bids. She puts in a number, and it comes back straight away as denied. Thinking for a second, she throws another figure, higher, and once again, it comes back denied. When she glances at me in silent question, I nod my head in agreeance. We have a limit for these things, but sometimes, just sometimes, we have to go over it. Maria smiles when she wins the first one, but the second one seems to be trickier. We stand and wait in a closed-off area—each buyer gets privacy to bid. It's all incredibly top secret, and they do a great job at keeping it that way.

"Got them." Maria smiles proudly.

"Good. Go and collect them."

Maria nods before she walks off. I go to leave, and I see Burke, a collector of all things beautiful, step outside the same time I do.

He smirks as he sees me, heading in my direction. "It's been a while, Jake. I've heard stories you have been buying overseas." I look to Captain, who is waiting for me, then I turn back to Burke, who's dressed in heavy black boots and black jeans with a white shirt.

"Rumors," I tell him.

"Are they true?" he asks.

"Does it matter?"

He shakes his head and pulls a cigarette out of his pocket, and lights it. "I guess not, just beware. Talk is circulating, Jake. And the talk isn't good." He tips his head to me and turns to leave. "You have a good night, Jakey."

For fuck's sake. I grind my teeth as he walks away.

"Trouble," Captain says, watching him as well.

"That he is." I already knew this though, so it's no great surprise he is making trouble.

But my main concern is a redhead who won't leave my fucking mind.

CHAPTER 10
Date me before you fuck me
ORIANA

It's been almost two months of doing nothing.

I'm not used to being this way.

I thought I was doing okay at the three-week mark and decided it was time to look for work. Then I got divorce papers in the mail. That knocked me down for a few more weeks.

It's as if Kyler didn't even care. Like the last ten years meant nothing. The asshole didn't even fight for me.

That hurt the most.

And then the real kicker came when he showed up to a recent movie event with another woman on his arm. And he kissed her. Kissed her on the lips as if he enjoyed it. He stopped kissing me on the lips out in public years ago.

I haven't left this house since I moved in, not wanting the tabloids to get a photograph of me.

I can imagine the headline now...

Oriana Now Homeless

TECHNICALLY, I'm not homeless, but I just may look it, unfortunately.

Today is my birthday, and Simone has made plans. I tried to get out of it—you know, because of a divorce and everything—but she just brushed it off.

Harvey is back today for my birthday before he flies off again later this week. He's always in town for my birthday because it's a tradition and one I am thankful for. I'm not sure how I got this far without him.

"Hey." Harvey walks in the door, stopping and staring at me as he approaches. "What the hell is going on with you?"

"What?"

I'm standing in my pajamas with a coffee in hand.

"You look like shit. Truly. Do you plan to go out looking like that?"

My mouth falls open at his words. "I look great," I say back.

"You look like a homeless person."

"I do not." I scoff, spilling the coffee. He only laughs as he goes into the kitchen and makes his own coffee.

"You should call a hairdresser and possibly a magician," he suggests.

"Ha ha," I deadpan, heading to the shower. The doorbell rings, but I don't turn back to answer it. "That will be Simone. Let her in, please."

"Simone is annoying," Harvey grumbles.

"I can hear you," Simone yells from the other side of the door.

I laugh as I jump in the shower, wash my hair, scrub my body, and shave every inch of me that I haven't touched in months. When I'm done, I climb out and wrap a towel around myself before I step out of the bathroom to find silence. I look around the corner and see Harvey standing between Simone's legs as she sits on the counter with her arms around his neck.

They're kissing.

Oh.

Oh.

Okay.

When did that happen?

And why did that happen?

"Is this a thing now?" I casually ask, and they pull apart quickly.

Simone falls from the counter, straightens her skirt, and smiles at me.

"You're looking human again," my brother says, ignoring my question and avoiding eye contact.

"Do you do this often?" I ask, taking in their guilty expressions.

"No," they answer in unison.

"Well, you know I'm always happy to cancel and stay in. You two can go out," I offer.

"That's not happening. It's your birthday, and the makeup artist will be here soon," Simone says.

"I don't need a makeup artist," I tell them, then turn to go to my room.

"Oh, you so do," Harvey yells.

"Stop kissing my best friend," I scream out, shutting my door and falling onto my bed.

The door opens, and I don't bother to see who it is when the bed dips next to me and Simone touches my shoulder. "You need to start living again. He has clearly moved on. You need to do the same."

"Ten years, Simone. I gave that man ten years. How?" I groan into my pillow.

"You fell for all his charms hook, line, and sinker." She slaps my ass.

"That's not happening again. The next man will fall hook, line, and sinker for me."

Simone stands and crosses the room, then rifles through my closet before she lands on a black dress and throws it at me.

"That's your comeback dress. The makeup artist is almost here, so get dressed while I make your new favorite...margaritas."

"I will get out of bed for margaritas," I tell her, smiling.

"Damn right you will." She bounces out the door as I get up. I go to pick some underwear, but this dress will show panty lines, so I look for my Spanx, but somehow, I've lost them in the move. I ended up having to rent a storage unit to store all my big things to make room in Harvey's place and only kept all the things I would need in the short term.

So, I slip the dress on, without panties or Spanx, and slide my feet into a pair of heels. When I step out of my room, Simone is opening the front door for the makeup artist.

I guess we're going out.

HARVEY INVITED A FEW FRIENDS, and Simone has been eyeing him all night. I've had maybe three too many margaritas but stopped when my fourth was put in front of me.

It's weird celebrating a birthday without Kyler. Not that he did much for it anyway, but after ten years, the empty place by my side is noticeable.

My only requests tonight were that we don't go to the club we went to last time, and I buy all my own drinks. Hence why the fourth is sitting in front of me untouched. It's not so much that I don't want to drink, I just would rather not risk being in another situation like the last time we went out ever again if I can help it.

"Just go up to him," I tell her with an eye roll.

Simone's eyes flick to mine. "What?" She tries to play dumb.

"All you've been doing is staring at my brother. Go talk to him." I wave a hand in his direction, which makes him look our way.

He raises a brow in question, but I dismiss him with a shake of my head.

"I'll be fine sitting here. It's fun to watch drunk people."

"Are you sure it's okay if I go over there? I felt bad last time leaving you..." She trails off, and I know she is feeling uneasy and she shouldn't.

I reach for a strand of my hair and start twirling.

"It's fine, trust me. Plus, you aren't leaving this time without me, are you?" I confirm.

"No, tonight is *your* night."

"Good. So go kiss face with my brother." I cringe slightly, and we both share a laugh. "And I would *not* like to hear anything about it."

"I'll sit with her."

We both turn at the voice coming from behind us. A shiver races through me as I gaze up at a pair of eyes I haven't seen for a few months. Charcoal gray orbs stare back at me, and I wonder if he's been to hell and back because his eyes tell me he has.

"Go. I'll be fine," I tell her again.

Simone stands and saunters off, straight to my brother.

Jake studies me, his eyes framed by long, thick lashes. Really, it's unfair he has those naturally while I have to contend with glue-ons. He makes no move to sit, just looms behind me.

"Is this one of your places as well?" I ask.

"Yes," he answers, not giving me any more information.

My eyes flick around the club, trying to avoid eye contact before I glance back at him. This time, I take him in more fully. His shoes are black and shiny, his slacks are matte black, matched with a dark gray button-up shirt with the sleeves rolled up his forearms.

His hair is shorter than it was the last time I saw him. And those eyes lock on me and read things about me I don't want anyone else to see.

This man has seen me at my absolute worst.

And he stands there as someone who knows my inner thoughts.

"Do you plan to stand there all night?" Maybe he'll make me less nervous sitting beside me? Actually, probably not.

"Care to take a walk?" He looks down at my drink. "Since you have only had three since you arrived." I had one at home before we left too, but he doesn't need to know that.

"You're counting my drinks? Have you been watching me this whole time?" I ask, annoyed.

"Yes, since the minute you walked in. Now, come. I can tell you would rather not be here. My office is out back." I turn to where my brother and Simone are shaking hips and locking lips as they dance without a care in the world for anyone but themselves.

Kyler and I were once like that.

I mentally slap myself for thinking of him.

I turn my attention to Jake but make no move to get up, but he is now standing closer, offering me one of his hands. "Consider this one of our dates."

"Dates?" I ask.

"Yes, you owe me. Or have you forgotten?"

I kind of did, but I don't tell him that.

It's not that he is forgettable. It's that my life has been a shitstorm, and I'm still trying to work it all out. No one tells you that when you leave your husband, your entire world will change or that it's the small things you'll miss like seeing his things in the shower or making two cups of coffee every morning.

I glance at Jake's hand—it's perfect, sexy, manicured, and strong—and he's waiting for me to take it. Reaching out, I place my hand in his and stand. He doesn't let go as we start walking, and I can't say I dislike the way it feels. Though he's powerful in his stance, the way he leads me is gentle and comforting. As we come to a stop at the bar, he turns to look at me.

"Would you like me to make you a drink?"

I don't know why, but I nod my head. He pulls me over to the end of the bar, lifts the hinged section, and glides through. All the bartenders offer him their help, but he simply shrugs it off as he grabs the right glass and returns to where he left me standing. He puts it all out in front of me—the tequila, salt, lime, and Cointreau, then starts to make it so I can see everything he's doing.

The thing is though, I know he's not doing it to impress me. He's doing it because I don't trust my drink being made anymore. It took me three hours to drink the three margaritas I ordered, and I watched them make every drink and never let it leave my sight.

I smile up at him as he focuses on mixing the ingredients and rimming the glass with salt.

"You're good at that."

"It's not the only thing I'm good at." He winks as he shakes it all before he pours it into the glass and hands it over to me.

I lift it, take a sip, and can't help but moan. "Gosh, this is amazing."

"So was that." Before I can ask him what he's talking about, he is out from behind the bar and reaching for my hand again.

A guy opens the door at the back and lets us in.

His office is small with one desk and a seat on either side. Nothing hangs on the walls indicating that it's anyone's or making it someone's personal space. I scan the space as he goes over to a bank of black screens and touches something. The screens light up, showing different camera angles within the club.

"Do you usually watch from back here?"

"No, I was leaving when I saw you walk in." I gape at him.

"I've been here for two hours," I say incredulously.

"I know." He sits down and nods his head to the empty seat in front of him. "So, about our date."

"I just don't think I'm ready," I tell him, my heart beating a little faster.

"I'm not asking you to marry me, Oriana. I'm asking for something you owe me, and I always collect my debts." His fingers tap on his desk, one by one, and I sit there mesmerized by it before I blurt out, "Do you bring other women back here?"

"Yes." He doesn't hesitate.

"And what do you do with them?" I look at my drink for some reason.

Do I really want to know the answer?

"No, I do not make them drinks. They usually suck my cock." My eyes go wide, and he places his elbows on the desk, leaning forward. "Does that bother you? Someone else on their knees in front of me, her head bobbing up and down as she sucks my cock, draining it with her perfect lips, sucking me dry?"

I go to stand on impulse, my heels digging into the floor as I do, shock vibrating through me like a steam train. But something inside me, something I can't make sense of, makes me sit straight back down.

He smirks. "Tell me, Oriana. Did that selfish husband of yours ever give you a good time? Have you ever been put on a desk and had your pussy ravished?"

My cheeks go red at his words. I feel them becoming brighter and brighter with the heat. The warmth of my skin is a rush I haven't felt in too long. "Oriana." He says my name and my eyes snap up to meet his. "Have you?"

I don't know why my answer leaves my lips, but somehow, he makes it. "No," I reply quietly.

He sits back in his chair, nodding.

"Has he ever tasted you?" My hand lifts to my hair, and I start twirling it with my finger.

"Yes," I tell him, and he nods. "But it's not his thing," I add with a slight shrug.

He scoffs. "It's every man's thing. Having a woman come undone by your mouth alone is a power trip. When she calls out your name, or even better, calls out for God. But the one you call when you scream for me, will be 'yes, Master,' right against my mouth." I cross my legs at the visual his words bring to my mind, my core tingling. "Would you like me to show you?"

CHAPTER 11
Just a taste

JAKE

er cheeks are red.

They almost match her hair.

I didn't plan to bring her in here to fuck her, but how can I resist when she sits there staring at me with those big doe eyes, looking fucking irresistible.

I let her be after the day I went to her brother's house.

Haven't even thought of bothering her. Until she walked—no, swayed her hips—into my club tonight. She wouldn't have known this place is mine and that's okay, but it didn't stop me from sitting here watching her.

I could see she felt awkward. She was eyeing her drink as if she were afraid something might be slipped into it. I wouldn't let that happen to her again, especially when I am around.

Grinding my molars, I study her.

She can't seem to form words.

Did I stun her so badly she doesn't know how to speak?

"I bet you taste as good as you look," I say, standing. "I bet your sweet cunt is wet right now. Am I right?"

Her eyes grow even wider, and I realize it's the words I use. Striding to the door, I touch the lock. "You feel safe with me, right? If I locked this door, you wouldn't be scared?" Her pretty eyes flick to the lock. "Words, Oriana," I snap at her.

"I am scared of you," she whispers.

I don't lock the door. Instead, I let my hand drop.

"Why?" I want to know because her reaction to me is anything but frightened. It's quite the opposite. The way she fidgets in her seat as she keeps on crossing and uncrossing her legs as if she is unsure. Her eyes as they track me.

"You say these vulgar things."

"Do they turn you on?" I ask. Her hand goes to her hair, and she starts twirling it again. "Oriana."

"Will you stop saying my name like that," she snaps.

"Like what?"

"Like you want to say it in other contexts."

"You mean like I want to say it as you suck my

cock?" She bites her lip. "Or you want me to say it when my head disappears under that dress you're wearing and I tear your panties off?"

She throws her head back and laughs. Her hand that was in her hair falls to her chest, and she giggles— it's cute, really. This is not the answer I was looking for, but I appreciate it all the same.

Most women don't giggle when I tell them what I want to do.

But this treasure, she's delicate.

A little feisty when she wants to be, but delicate at the same time. The world hasn't swallowed her whole yet and spat her out.

When she's calmed down, I look at her quizzically.

"What was funny?"

She sucks in a breath as she wipes her eyes and looks at me. "I'm not wearing any panties."

When I say I did not expect her reply, I mean... I. Did not. Fucking. Expect it. I march back to the door and lock it.

"What are you doing?" she asks, no fear in her voice, just curiosity.

"You have no panties on," I state.

"I didn't do it on purpose. Well, I did, but only because I didn't want to show any panty lines."

"But you told me," I say. "Which is just as good as spreading your legs right now and showing me."

"I'm not going to show you," she bites back, crossing her legs.

"You aren't?" I smirk. "Are you so sure?" Stepping closer, I lean down to her ear, then breathe on it before I whisper, "How wet are you right now? If you stood up, would it leak down your thighs?"

"Oh my God."

"No, we discussed this. I prefer my women to call me Master."

She turns so our faces are touching, our lips close to each other. "Is that what you get other women to call you? Master?" She raises a brow, and my eyes fall to her lips, coated in red to match her hair.

"Yes, they all do, eventually."

"I'm not all women, Jake." She licks her bottom lip, and her tongue touches my lips ever so slightly with how close we are.

"No, I guess you aren't." I pull away and drop to my knees. Oriana tries to push the chair back, but it's stuck. When I touch her calf, she jolts in her seat.

"What are you doing?" she screeches.

Dropping my hand on her foot, I lift it. "Admiring my shoes on your feet." She lets me lift it, and I smile. From my kneeling position, I can see up her dress. "And you are wet."

Then she surprises me again.

She spreads her legs.

CHAPTER 12
Two can play that game
ORIANA

He thinks he's clever, but two can play this game.

"Oriana." I hear the hint of a warning in his tone. He's clenching his jaw, and his hand on my calf stills before gripping it a little tighter. "I can see your cunt."

"Don't use that word," I scold. "I don't like that word."

He licks his lips. A man is on his knees in front of me, and it makes me feel powerful.

"Cunt is a beautiful word. Society has made it foul. It should just be a dirty word, but the way people use it makes it seem wrong. Stop thinking of it as a foul word and see it for what it is, just a word that has little meaning." His gaze drops to between my legs. I spread them wider for him, and his hand on my calf moves upward until he reaches my knee, then he pauses. "You should probably stop showing me your cunt, Mrs. Lavender, unless you plan for me to devour it." The use of my married name coming out of his mouth does something to me.

Maybe it's the margaritas kicking in, or maybe it's just him.

I do something I didn't even know I could do.

Sex with Kyler was great. I loved our sex life—when we had one. But whatever this is, it isn't just sexy, it is intoxicating.

Lifting my leg, I place my heel on his shoulder. He grins, his eyes on mine, before they trail down my body to what I'm offering up to him.

"Show me what you got," I half-whisper, barely believing those words came out of my mouth.

"It's not every day I get on my knees for a woman."

"How often?" I ask.

Jake's hand skims my knee before it slowly inches upward. "Never."

And I believe him.

I do.

I hate that I do.

Am I that gullible?

I also think he isn't a man who lies often.

"I'm waiting." I raise an eyebrow.

"You are. I can smell you. Did you know?" His words make me tense, questioning my sudden confidence. "You smell fucking amazing." The compliment, and how he says it, low and assertive, has me swallowing roughly.

Damn! I'm enjoying this *way too much*.

Both of his strong hands now touch my inner thighs, and in one swift movement, he pushes my legs as wide as they can go.

"This won't be a thing between us. Just sex," I tell him as he leans in.

"A date. I agree."

"Sex?" I ask.

"Yes, a date where we fuck. You still owe me one more, if I remember correctly."

"So I do..."

He moves forward, his lips touching my inner thigh, and air leaves my lungs in a rush of what feels like relief.

A kiss.

Just a kiss.

And I already feel like putty in his hands.

Am I really going to do this? Am I going to let this man I barely know put his head between my legs and taste me?

Yes. Yes, I am. Because that's what a woman my age would do. She would have fun sleeping around, especially after only being with the same person for almost my entire life, and right now, I deserve this.

This is all new to me.

A man on his knees in front of me is new.

Kyler would have never wanted to do this.

Jake moves even closer, his lips tickling and lingering all over my skin.

Nervousness shoots through me, and I think for a second I should stop. Stop this while I can.

Then he slides a finger up my dress and touches my clit. I jump at the contact, but he's fast, holding my hips down with his other hand while his lips stay on my skin.

"Oriana." He looks up at me.

"Hmm..." I say, peering down at him.

"Tell me you're okay."

"I'm okay."

He smirks before licking his way up my leg until he reaches the juncture of my thighs. When his hot mouth skims the outside of my lips, I yelp and moan at the same time. He doesn't stop, and I'm not sure I want him to, as he continues to hold me in place with one hand while the other slides forward, and I feel his finger enter me. Jake's pace starts slow, his finger leaving and entering in languid push and pulls as his hot mouth latches onto my clit, licking in small circles, making me woozy.

What is this?

And why am I loving it?

His movements are perfect. It is as if he's taking his time, having his favorite dessert.

Maybe tonight I am exactly that—his favorite dessert.

I always thought maybe it was something about me that made Kyler not want to do this. Sometimes I thought, *do I smell?* Is that a thing? Was he turned off by my smell or taste? But when I look down at Jake, as my ass hangs off the chair and his head stays buried between my legs, I know it wasn't me. Jake is treating me as if I am a goddess.

A small flash jumps into my mind.

Of course, he would be good at this. The man owns a sex club, after all.

His tongue moves and does this thing to my clit that makes my hips buck beneath him, and all thoughts disappear.

Jake holds me down, not giving me space to move, and keeps on doing it while his other hand works his fingers in and out of me.

I can feel the build. It's high above me, like I'm trying to reach something I didn't ask for but now need more than anything. Helplessly and desperately climbing for it.

"Tell me you love the way I..." lick, "taste your cunt." His hot breath tickles me, and I push myself more into his face.

Is that bad? I feel like I need him closer, want more of him everywhere.

"Needy cunt this is." He pulls away, and a sound echoes through the room as a sting shoots through my private parts, and when I look down, I realize he slapped me.

Oh. My. God.

Before I can even think of saying anything, his face is back between my legs and making me thankful I'm not standing. I start riding his face, my hips rolling on the chair when he pulls away again. He stays on his knees, removing his hand from between my legs. Then he pushes my dress up around my ass and stands me up. Sliding one hand down my calf to my ankle, he lifts my leg.

I grab him to steady myself from falling as he puts it over his shoulder. And before I can say a word, his mouth is back on me, and my hands find their way to his hair and grip.

Holy hell.

Holy hell.

His finger slides inside me, followed by a second, and I have to remember I am now on my feet so I don't fall.

"Such a sweet cunt," he says into my flesh. "I want you to come. When my mouth touches you, fuck it and come. Do you understand?" he commands.

When I do nothing he is more forceful with his words. "Oriana, do you understand?"

I nod because it's the only response I can give before he smirks and lowers his face between my legs. His tongue slides up and down before it goes back to my clit.

His fingers push a little deeper, and I grip his hair tighter, as his tongue moves slowly and explores me.

Perfectly marking me; making me experience something I've only heard girls whisper about.

It's everything.

Everything.

"That's it," he croons as I come undone with trembling legs and a choked scream. And before I can move or even fall, the chair is back, and I'm dropping onto it.

That was...

He stands, and my eyes fall to his pants as he rearranges himself and turns and walks to the door, smiling.

"Our date is over. It looks like your friend is looking for you." Jake pulls the door open, and a man is standing there with his back to it. "It was a pleasure, Oriana." He waves for me to leave. "Until next time."

I manage to stand and pull my dress down before I walk up to him.

I've never had this happen.

Am I meant to say something?

Do I say thanks for the great things your mouth did?

Or do I just leave without a word?

I think I'm going to go with the latter option.

Smiling, I step out the door and don't look back. I spot Simone straight away—her back is to me, but I don't miss her.

Harvey is looking around on the dance floor, and when his eyes finally find me, he smiles. "Where have you been?" he asks with a touch of worry.

"I needed some air. Are you ready?"

They both nod.

When we walk outside, the cold air hits my skin. I turn to my right and see Jake standing at a car, another woman in front of him, her hand on his chest as she talks to him.

"Do you know him?"

I look over to Simone, who is watching me.

"No." I shake my head as Harvey hails a cab. I try not to look back, but I can't help myself.

"Isn't that the guy from earlier?" Simone asks, squinting her eyes to get a better look.

"I don't think so." I reach up and touch my hair. When I glance back, I see Jake has his hand on the lady's hip, not gripping her, just holding her there. He looks past her to me, and he smirks before he winks and climbs into the car with her following behind him.

Should I have asked if he was single?

That would have been smart, right?

Oh gosh, I never want to be known as a home-wrecker. That's not who I am. And with that though, I start to feel physically ill. Hurrying into an alley, I empty my stomach everywhere. Simone is there instantly, her hand rubbing gentle circles on my back.

"Did you have too much to drink?" she asks with genuine sincerity.

I wipe my mouth as the car drives away with Jake inside.

"No, I just felt—"

"Okay, well, let's get you home."

I simply nod as we get into the cab.

Simone and Harvey chat on the way home, and I think of what I just did and how good it felt.

How can something so good be so wrong?

And why am I excited to see him again?

But first, I have to ensure he isn't married.

Because that is a no-no for me.

It is a line I will never cross.

When I look down at my legs, I wonder why I didn't ask to begin with.

CHAPTER 13

You can call me boss

JAKE

"You like her," Captain says, and I smile at him as the doors open. It's late, and we are expecting both of the purchased girls to arrive tonight.

Maria stands next to me, iPad in hand, as she works on something.

Captain looks around, checking as some patrons start to leave.

"I do not. I like no one."

"You like me," Captain replies, nodding his head to the side. "And Maria."

Maria simply nods, too entrenched in what her iPad is telling her.

"And yet I would fuck neither of you."

"But you would fuck her." I grind my teeth at his words because he doesn't know how close to the truth that is. "Or you already did."

"My cock has not entered her pussy," I tell him honestly. "Not that you need to know that."

"Who else are you going to talk about it to? We're your only friends," Captain adds.

"One of you is family. The other I pay a lot to be loyal." I look to Captain. "Did you forget that?"

"Nope. But a pay raise wouldn't hurt."

Maria coughs next to me, trying to hide her laughter.

"Some say a bullet may not hurt either, but I beg to differ."

"Tomayto, tomahto," he says, and I shake my head at him.

The women we bought a week ago have been in rehabilitation, which is the first step for them. Some need longer, and some need just enough time to get clean. Maria checked on them today, and they seem to be doing okay. Only time will tell. Some of the women I buy go straight back to the life I pulled them from, while others are glad to be free and want to live life any way they can as long as they get to choose.

Most of my girls are that way.

I buy them to save them, but in return, I give them a job. Here. Some who are not comfortable playing with customers serve the drinks or have other jobs in the club. But there are many who are more than happy to earn extra cash.

It's usually couples who frequent the club.

We do get some singles, but it's mostly couples wanting to explore different options.

My girls, and guys, give them that.

I have rescued men as well. They can be tricky to keep in this field, but some stay loyal.

I didn't start off owning a sex club. I began investing in dance clubs, then moved to purchase my own. When that grew boring, I ventured into the sex side.

Sex makes money.

It's a billion-dollar industry.

From sex shops, to books, to strip clubs.

Sex sells.

Everyone knows it.

But in this town, to have something like that, you need protection. And that form of protection for me is Keir. A mafia boss who's more than happy for he and his men to own a percentage. In return, they do nothing but add their name to my establishment.

It works.

No one fucks with something the mafia own unless they want to be six feet under.

Despite not owning the club outright, I run it as if I do. They have no say—it was in our contract, and it works for all of us.

Some of his men are clientele.

I raise my head as the door to my office opens. Two girls walk in, dressed differently from the first night I saw them. The blonde is more eager, while the other one, who was too busy scratching her arm the last time I saw her, looks like she has some nice color back in her face.

My establishment has one rule—no drugs.

It's non-negotiable.

People fuck.

They can drink.

They can spank.

They can play out almost any fantasy here.

But if you bring drugs into my establishment, you are out.

That goes for my workers as well.

"Maria has explained to you what is expected?" I ask them. The blonde fidgets nervously as she focuses her gaze on the floor. "You don't have to do anything you don't want to do. It's your choice."

"We owe you?" the one with the scarred arms asks.

"You do. You can work here, earn a wage, and I'll take my cut. Or you will find another way to pay me back."

"I can't have sex with anyone," she says and looks at the blonde.

"I will," the blonde replies.

Maria nods. Happy with both answers.

"Nothing will be forced on you. All my employees have every opportunity to say no to any customer they choose. This is a place of fun...and money. Do you both understand?" They nod, and I look at the blonde. "Maria will set you up with shopping and salon day and whatever else you will need." Looking at the other girl, I tell her, "The same for you. The house you are both in, do you like it?"

They nod.

"The girls are nice," the blonde says. "It feels safe."

"It is. No one would dare come in here and fuck with what is mine." One of the girls puts her head down as a small smile touches her lips while the other smiles at me. They probably aren't used to safety.

"It's your first night, so you can stay behind the bar and get a feel for the club, then you can decide."

Again they nod, and I watch as Maria walks them out.

"So, do you plan to see her again?" Captain asks, sitting on the free seat.

"Yes."

"Then you do like her."

"She owes me one more date, and that's it."

"You think after one more date that you'll be done?" He throws his head back and laughs while clapping his chest hard. "You crack me up. You stay away from women so you don't get attached, and yet you run a business full of women who you help. They all may see you as a badass, but we know you are a softie."

"A softie who is going to fire your ass and set your beloved car on fire if you don't fucking get out of my office."

He stands, waving a hand at me while saying with a chuckle, "Okay, boss."

CHAPTER 14

Not my home, bitch

ORIANA

I found a job.

I've been applying for weeks for pretty much anything and everything and finally, something came through the other night. I didn't see it until I woke up the following morning, but I smiled as I read the email.

Congratulations, you have been awarded the position of...

I WON THE POSITION.

All by myself.

I wonder if they called Kyler for a reference.

I did put him down as a referee and sent him a message that I was doing so, but he never replied.

Does it bother him that I'm looking for work? He was more than happy to have me do everything for *him*.

I had an interview for this one over the phone, and a Zoom call as well. I wasn't sure I would get the position, as I don't have much experience in managing multiple people, but what a surprise. I guess when they find out you were a personal assistant to one of the biggest stars in the world, that helps.

I start on Monday, helping an agency of personal assistants to the stars. We hire and assign each one individually.

Working for myself and not for my husband feels good.

I jump out of bed to go tell Harvey the good news, but when I get to his room, I find he isn't there. Deciding to go out for breakfast by myself seems like the best plan. Celebrate by myself.

After dressing in jeans and a cropped shirt, I put on a large hat, sunglasses, and a pair of boots. It doesn't take me long to arrive at a local café that makes the best breakfast. When I sit down, my phone starts ringing. When I look at it, Kyler's face flashes on my screen.

I forgot to change it.

I bite the inside of my cheek as I stare at his face, a

picture of him one night after we went out. He's looking up at me as I snap it from two steps above him. He was waiting for me, and I told him to smile. Instead, he chose not to, holding out his hand and saying we should go.

I love that picture. It's a mixture of *my wife is impossible* and the hidden smirk that lingered, which told me he was thinking *my wife is cute*.

Maybe I made all that up in my head.

But I still loved him either way.

The question right now is, why is he calling me?

My birthday was yesterday, and I didn't hear a word from him. So why now?

I'm almost too afraid to answer, so I sit there and let it ring out. Not touching it in case I accidentally press accept.

When the screen goes black, a sigh of relief leaves me.

Then it starts again vibrating and loudly chirping with his face looking at me.

The waiter places my food in front of me. A stack of fancy syrupy pancakes, with cotton candy sprinkled all over them with berries and gold flakes. But I'm too busy looking at my phone to appreciate the yummy food in front of me.

When it stops the second time, I reach out to switch my phone off. But before I can, he calls again.

Nope.

Nope.

Nope.

Why would he do that?

When I finally have it powered down, I slide it into my bag and eat my pancakes. They don't taste the same as I hoped they would. I think because now I'm not so excited about everything. Kyler has a habit of spoiling my mood and even though I didn't pick the phone up, I still feel like whatever he was going to say has soured my state of mind. I'm disappointed that my day has been ruined. Goddamn him.

I eat half the pancakes, drink my coffee, and then decide to leave. No point sitting here dwelling. Why can't he leave me alone? I know I have to get on with my life, and I am trying so hard to do that. One unanswered phone call from Kyler, and I am back at square one.

Turning my phone back on as I walk out the door of the café, multiple messages come through one after the other. All from Kyler.

Kyler: Call me.

Kyler: Now.

Kyler: Oriana, this isn't a joke.

Kyler: Call me.

Kyler: This is urgent.

I DEBATE NOT CALLING him back. He does *not* deserve to talk to me, but if it's urgent, how can I not? It would be irresponsible, right?

So pressing call, he answers on the first ring.

"You need to come home. *Now.*"

"I'm almost home," I answer.

"You are?" I look up at Harvey's house and smile.

"Yep."

I hear rustling before he says, "I'm standing out front. Where are you coming from?"

My feet freeze as I look at Harvey's place, but I don't see anyone there.

"You're here?"

"What?" he asks. "Are you at home or not?"

"Which home?" I ask, confused. "I only have one home, it's with Harvey."

"No, Oriana, it's with me. And the home we created together."

"You are mistaken. Now, what do you want?"

"Harvey hasn't moved?" I hear the sound of a car door slamming.

"No, why?" My feet are frozen in place as I stare at the front door of Harvey's home.

"I'm on my way." Then he hangs up.

I could go elsewhere. Hide from him. But why should I be the one doing that? Kyler is the one who fucked me over. He is the one who stopped loving me. Granted, it takes two, but there is always one who checks out first.

And it was him.

Definitely him.

I persevered for so long, put up with so much, only to find he never cared about me.

I'm still standing in front of Harvey's house when I see Kyler's car pull up. He opens the driver's door and gets out.

"Can we go inside?" He nods to the house.

"No." He looks shocked by my answer but nods his head. "Why are you here, Kyler? You sent divorce papers. You've moved on. So why?" He scratches the back of his head as he lifts his phone with his other hand.

That's when he presses play.

And a voice I know well comes through the speaker.

"Tell me you love the way I taste your cunt."

Followed by my moan.

My hands fly to my mouth as Kyler stands there, red-faced and angry. I lean over to see the screen, but it's only a voice message.

How did—

"You're fucking Jake King?" he asks with a huff. "Of all people..."

His remark and the way he says it makes me fume.

"I can sleep with whomever I want."

"So you admit to fucking him?"

"How did you get that?" I ask, my face warm with embarrassment.

"Jake sent it to me. Wanted me to know what I was missing out on." His jaw grinds back and forth. "And to thank me for giving you up." I bite my lip and his eyes lock on me. "Did you enjoy it?"

I know he's expecting me not to answer, but I do anyway. "Yes, very much so. He made me see stars with only his mouth." I smirk, reveling in this asshole's reaction.

He drops his phone from his hand, shocked and gaping.

"It's not something you ever did for me," I add.

"No, it's not. Are you saying you didn't like our sex life?"

"It was very..." I search for the right word. "Vanilla." I know by the look on his face he doesn't like the use of that word. *Would any man?*

"You need to stop seeing him. He has ties to the mafia. You know that, right?"

I didn't, but I guess now I do.

"So?"

He shakes his head and leans down to pick up his phone. "I've thought about this…about us, a lot. I think this is over, and you should move back home."

"I am home," I tell him. "Do you know what yesterday was?"

His brow rises. "No?"

"My birthday." I swing around and stomp up the stairs to Harvey's house. What nerve this man has, standing there demanding what *he* wants and not even knowing he missed my birthday.

"Oriana."

"I hate my name when you say it," I whisper.

"You don't," he says, and he's right. I don't. But I thought it would be good to say it, to make him feel like shit. I feel him come up behind me and he whispers in my ear, "I miss you." His breath tickles my neck before he kisses it.

A shiver takes over my body.

But do you want to know what?

It's not the type of shiver it should be.

Kyler doesn't make me feel giddy inside, electrified, not the way Jake does.

"You should go," I manage to say. "Go to your new plaything. I saw you two kissing. Do you even remember the last time you kissed me on the lips, Kyler?" I pull back and step away. Turning to look at him, his mouth is open and his eyes are wide. "You don't have a single clue. See, this is why we are no longer together. We don't work, and that's okay. One day, someone *will* work for me."

"He won't be it, Oriana. Don't go down that rabbit hole."

"I'm already down there, and it's more than a little bit of fun." I smile, completely uncaring of his opinion or his image. "Say hello to your new boo for me." Opening the door, I slide inside and lock it behind me, then go to my room before I call Jake. I start pacing when he doesn't pick up straight away, but just before I hang up and try again, his voice comes through, sounding sleepy.

"What?"

"You!" I yell into the phone.

"Fuck, woman, it's early, and some of us work all night," he grumbles.

"I don't care. You, you, you…"

"Asshole?" I can hear the smile in his voice as he finishes my sentence.

"Yes, that. How dare you send that recording to Kyler. What were you thinking?"

"I was thinking that little Mr. Goody Two-Shoes needs a reality check. He lost someone amazing. I bet he tried to win you back, didn't he? But you, my dear, are too clever to fall for that, right?"

"Right." I give an eye roll because how the hell does he know me so well this soon.

"Tonight, dress sexy. I'm taking you to my sex club."

"The one where—"

"Yes, the very same. You will be safe. Consider this our last date."

"Date?"

"Yes, Oriana. One where I plan for you to suck my cock. Maybe I'll even have a taste of that sweet pussy again. You never know."

I smirk at the thought of his mouth back down there, my thighs clenching as I imagine my lips on him this time.

"Oriana."

"Yes?"

"What did I say I like to be called?"

"Master," I reply firmly, feeling tingly all over.

"Yes. Now say it again."

We're both silent for a beat.

And then I do it.

Why? Lord knows.

"Master." There is no hesitation in my voice when I say it—it's straight begging.

"For that, you will get something special." He hangs up, and I'm left feeling confused.

I walk into my bedroom, lie on my bed, and watch *Grey's Anatomy* for the rest of the day until a knock sounds at my door, alerting me to a delivery.

After retrieving the delivery and tipping the drivers, I walk back to my room. Opening the box, a pair of panties fall out, and in those panties is a small black item in the front. I study them for a moment and then see the note.

Wear them tonight.
X Jake.

SLIDING THEM ON, I step up to my full-length mirror and take a photograph, being sure not to get my face in the image.

I send it to Jake with the caption... *Why these?*

His reply is instant.

Jake: Fuck. Now my cock is hard.
Keep them on until I take them
off you.

I SMILE as I read his text.

That is, until Kyler rings me again. Throwing my phone, I go back to bed and watch more trashy television until I have to leave.

For a date.

With Jake.

I hope to come again.

And again.

And again.

Who is this new Oriana?

I like her.

CHAPTER 15
Nice to meet you, let's fuck
JAKE

When she walks in, I see her on the screen in my office, the sky-high pink heels I gave her on her feet again. She stands at the entrance of the club alone and looking nervous.

Calling the hostess, she answers on the first ring.

"Give her a red wristband and bring her to the bar." I hang up, and the hostess greets Oriana, then places the red band on her wrist. Oriana looks at it in confusion before she asks what it's for. The hostess simply smiles and asks Oriana to follow her.

When they reach the bottom of the stairs, Oriana pauses, gaping as the beds come into view. Unlike the first time she was here, they aren't empty this time around.

People are everywhere. Fucking, touching, kissing.

Her eyes go wide, and the hostess motions toward

the bar. Oriana manages to tear her eyes away from the beds, and as she reaches the bar, she grips it for dear life while I grin as I sit there watching her.

The bartender offers her a drink, but she doesn't take it.

I wonder if she was a big drinker before the incident.

Oriana swings around, her back to the bar, and checks her surroundings. I get up from my chair and head out into the bar, stepping up behind her.

"A margarita to loosen you up?"

She turns to face me, and there is something in her eyes, but I'm not sure what.

"Are you the one making it?" she asks.

"I am."

"Well, then I'll say...*yes, please*."

I smile at her before I proceed to fix her drink. Truth be told, I had to Google how to make a margarita after I saw she had one.

"Why did you message my husband?" Oriana asks, not sounding as mad as she did earlier about it.

I stop at the salt and look up at her to answer. "He annoys me."

"How so?" She leans on the counter, her hands cupping her face, interest clear in her eyes.

"He let someone like you go. But I guess that's his own stupidity."

"You really know how to make a girl feel special," she replies sarcastically.

"It's what a man should do... Fuck her and treat her like a queen."

"And when you're done with me?" She lifts her brow.

"We will part on good terms, like all the other women I've fucked before you."

"We haven't fucked," she says as I shake the drink.

I stop. Then, with a sexy smirk, I say, "No, but let's change that tonight."

"I'm not sure I want to. You might record me again and send it to my husband."

"Maybe I will, maybe I won't." I shrug. "Does it matter? You know for a fact he won't share it with anyone because he wants his image to remain squeaky-clean perfect."

"I have divorce papers," she informs me. "So, soon I'll be officially divorced."

"Is that what you want?"

"I think so." Her forehead wrinkles.

"You should know so."

Her hand goes to her hair as I place the drink in front of her.

"Are you married?" she asks.

"No. I don't believe in marriage."

"Okay, did not expect that." She picks up her drink. "Who was the blonde that got into your car?"

"The blonde?" I question.

She nods. "You touched her hip." My lip quirks at the bit of jealously I know I am portraying.

"Oh, yes, that's Avani. She runs this place. You'll meet her soon."

She turns away and does a quick scan of the room before those rainforest green eyes find me again. "Why am I here?"

I press a button on the small device in my pocket, and her eyes go wide. She bites her lip and carefully places the drink down.

"Is that why I'm here?" she asks breathily.

"Do you not like it?" I ask, leaning toward her across the bar. She leans in too, her breathing picking up as her bottom wiggles on the stool.

"I..." She pauses, and her eyes flick to my lips. "You haven't kissed me yet."

"I haven't kissed your mouth," I confirm. "Would you like me to? I have kissed *other* places..." I grin as I glance down to where she is currently crossing her legs. "Are you comfortable?"

"I am."

Lies. I chuckle, then step out from behind the bar and walk around to where she is seated. I reach out and touch her red locks, which are down and free tonight in bouncy curls.

"Would you like me to kiss you now?" I ask, leaning in close yet not touching her. Her breaths tickle my lips as I wait. My hand finds her thigh, and I squeeze it before I press another button, making the buzzing sound even louder.

"Oh..." She shakes her head. "Y-yes, you can kiss me now." She leans in to kiss me, but I stop her with a finger to her lips. She parts them, and I press my finger into her mouth.

"Suck," I order.

She does, and my other hand glides up so I can press the vibrator harder against her clit. I pull my finger free from her mouth and slip it under her dress, where I pull her panties to the side before I place my wet finger on her clit. "So wet already. That's my girl." She moans as I slide my finger inside of her.

And then she seems to remember where we are, and her breathing stops as she looks around, panicked, before those eyes that I get lost in find mine. "People can see us," she whispers.

"Does it matter?" I ask, my tongue flicking out to run along my lips. She moves just a fraction, and as she does, I push my finger in deeper.

"How are you doing that?" she chokes out.

I nod down to my hand that's gripping her thigh.

Her brow raises, and she reaches for it, presses the button, and squeals as she puts it on the highest setting. I huff out a laugh at her reaction. I was planning on working her up to that.

"You should kiss me now," she says, leaning back in.

"I think you can wait."

"You are so mean." She groans, and I smile.

I lick her ear before I say, "No, baby, I'm going to make you come."

CHAPTER 16

Promises, promises

ORIANA

I believe his words.

He is indeed going to make me come.

As I move closer to him I bite the inside of my cheek, his finger inside of me still thrusting. I can't believe I'm doing this. Sitting in this place with his hand up my skirt and a vibrator in my panties.

What type of woman have I become?

He chuckles as I grip his shoulders, my nails digging in.

"That's my girl. Come for me, all around my fucking fingers. Milk them as if they were my cock."

I felt the orgasm break loose when he said, "That's my girl."

Why does that do it for me?

The best I was called from my ex-husband was "wife."

That was exciting at the beginning until it wasn't.

But "that's my girl"?

Does that ever get old? I believe not.

My grip loosens, and he removes his hand as I lay my head on his shoulder.

"Are you ready for me to show you around?" he asks.

I pull away from him and stand, righting my skirt and looking around to see if anyone has witnessed what just happened. I glance back to my drink, pick it up, and toss it all back before I nod. "Liquid courage."

"You don't need courage." He winks. "Just stamina."

I giggle, and he grips my hand, leading me from the bar. The blonde who I saw with him last night approaches us. She's dressed in a long, lacy shawl over the top of a lingerie set.

"Avani, what's wrong?" Jake asks before she can say anything.

"I want an expensive bag. Can that be my bonus this year? A real one, not a fake one." She smirks.

"What?" Jake says, clearly used to her strange ways.

"One of my clients had one, and I want one too."

"Then you need to find yourself a sugar daddy."

"As if." She rolls her eyes and gives me a small wave before she sashays off.

Jake looks back at me. "Avani is...*interesting*." I

can't help but giggle again at his description of her. He raises a brow.

"What?" I question.

"I like that sound." He shrugs, then leads me to another area. We move to the back, passing rooms and beds. Everyone wears a colored wristband, mostly yellow and green, while I am wearing a red one.

"What does red mean?" I ask.

"It means no one can touch you."

"You just did."

"That's different. No one *else* can touch you."

"So your rules don't apply to you?"

"They don't," he explains. "Yellow means you are interested but may not be ready; you're willing to watch and possibly play. Green means you are good for anything. So if someone comes up to you and they see you are wearing a green band, they know they can trust you won't straight up turn them down. It's comforting for people to know this information right away."

As we stop at the door, he touches a switch. The door becomes see-through, allowing us to view two couples, both playing with each other, having no idea we are standing there watching them.

He drops my hand and steps behind me. My eyes are locked on the room, where one of the women with blonde hair lies down and spreads her legs while the brunette drops her head between the other's legs. One of the guys starts to pump his cock over the first woman's mouth as she licks the tip of it, while the other guy goes behind the second woman. He positions her body and slides into her with ease, his expression full of ecstasy.

"Wow," I whisper.

"Do you like it?"

I glance back at him as he moves even closer to me, my back against his front now, and answer with one word, "Yes."

"I knew you would."

"You did?" I raise a brow.

"Yes. You just haven't had the opportunity to play with your other side yet."

"I like to play." His hand reaches around and slides up my dress, rubbing me through my panties.

"Are you ready for me yet?" he asks, and I nod and bite my lip. "Do you want to fuck like them?" He motions to the couples in the room. "I don't like to share, though."

"No sharing," I say, and his hands leave me.

"Good." He lifts me up and throws me over his shoulder. A squeal turns into a giggle, and then he slaps my ass. "Fuck, I love that sound."

I try to cover my mouth to stop giggling as he walks through a set of doors with me still on his shoulder, but my hand lands on his back for support. I grip his shirt and watch as it rides up, exposing the skin above his waistband.

"Do you do this a lot?" I ask.

He stops as we reach another door. Putting me down slowly, my body presses against his as he lowers me to my feet.

"No," he says as his gaze locks with mine. Then he reaches around me and opens the door, revealing a small room.

"Who sleeps in here?"

"This is where I crash if I'm tired."

From the doorway, I take in the tiny space. There's a single bed, but literally nothing else. No television, nothing.

"Are you nervous?" he asks, his breath tickling my neck.

I glance over my shoulder. "Should I be?"

He moves me into the room, then takes my purse and places it next to the bed before he steps away. "You should remove your clothes."

"All of them?"

"Yes."

"Will you?"

"Will I what?" he questions.

"Will you remove your clothes too?"

He smirks and nods. "If you want me to."

"Together," I say, feeling a bit more courageous.

This man gives me confidence. I'm not sure why or how—maybe it's in the way he looks at me—but when I'm with him, I feel *sexy.*

I lower the straps of my dress and let them drop down until they hit my arms. He watches me intently, his eyes never leaving mine in this small, secluded room.

This is a so-called date.

What happens when this is over?

Do we go our separate ways and never see each other again?

I try not to think about that. Whatever happens after, it's been fun.

He's made me see things about myself I didn't know were there.

Like what I enjoy in the bedroom—oral being a good example of that.

He stops me as I go to remove my heels.

"Leave them on while I fuck you, so you can dig them into my ass when you scream." I'm shocked at his words, though I shouldn't be. He isn't a man who gives you nice lovey-dovey words, his are dirty and laced with purpose, and I like them a lot.

Leaving my heels on, I drop my dress and step out of it, which puts me closer to Jake. So close that if I reached out now, I could touch him. His eyes take in my body, clad in only a pair of black panties.

"They can go."

I shimmy my panties down, and when I go to unhook them from my ankles, he snaps his fingers. "I want them back." He holds out his hand, and when I give them to him, he pockets them and smirks.

Now I stand before him naked.

He unbuttons his shirt and removes it with ease while I lick my lips. I can't help it. I always thought Kyler had a great body, but Jake? Well, Jake is something else. His body is perfection.

Toned, rigid, and hard.

I want to step forward and scrape my nails down his abs.

Jake removes his belt, holds it to the side, then smiles. "You should hold this." I take it from him, confused, then he removes his pants, and his cock springs free. It's hard and long.

And holy mother of all things sexy...

It's pierced.

"Oriana."

"Mm-hmm..." I can't raise my face to his because my eyes are locked on his.

He snaps his fingers, and I look up to see him smiling.

"You'll enjoy it."

"Will I? It looks like it will hurt." He shakes his head as he laughs.

"Trust me, you'll enjoy it." I nod my head, still a bit skeptical and anxious. "Do you want to touch it, Oriana? Because if you do, you need to get on your knees."

So that's exactly what I do, almost as if I've been spelled. I drop to my knees, and he steps behind me, taking the belt from my hand. "Put your hands together at your back." I do as he says, and then I feel him tie them together with his belt. "That's my girl," he whispers into my ear, kissing it before his tongue slides over my earlobe. A shiver takes hold of my body, and my breathing is heavy. He moves back in front of me, placing his rock-hard penis right in my face.

"I..."

"You want to taste it?" His hand goes to his penis, and he strokes it up and down while I watch, fascinated.

"Yes."

"That's my girl." As he moves forward, and I open my mouth, he leans down a little as my lips touch the tip where the piercing is located. I lick around it and feel him jolt against my lips.

"Fuck," he says on a groan.

Then I decide to hell with it, and cover the tip with my lips and suck him into my mouth. His hand grips my hair at the roots, and he pulls me back, then he bends down until he is kneeling in front of me and shakes his head. "That was bad, bad, bad." He picks me up and places me back on my feet.

"It didn't feel good?" I ask, confused.

"No, it felt fucking amazing. But you were trying to make me come with that sweet mouth of yours before I was ready." That statement has me feeling needy, wanting to taste him even more now.

His hand lands on my hip, gripping hard. "Now spread them." I do as he asks and spread my legs just a little as he gets back on his knees. My hands are still tied behind my back.

I feel his mouth on my clit, and my body goes into a state of readiness and happiness as he slides his tongue up and down, slow and torturous.

"Is your cunt hungry yet?"

I nod, biting my lip. He slides a finger into me, and I feel the orgasm building already. *How can he do that?* And then his mouth is gone. He's once again standing in front of me. "We can't make her sore yet. We need to play some more."

"Untie me," I beg. I want to run my hands over his chest, down to his...

"You have to ask nicely."

"Please, Jake," I shake my head "Master, will you untie me so I can touch you?"

"I suppose." I stay still as I feel him behind me, his hand sliding along my back and down to the top of my ass. It lingers there, not touching the belt that keeps my hands together. His lips caress my shoulder, then he moves them farther down, and down, until he's at my lower back. Then he bites my ass before he licks it, followed by a kiss. I feel him come close to the crack of my ass. He spreads my cheeks and slides a finger between them and straight up my...

"Holy—"

"Shit." I hear the smile in his voice as he interrupts what I was about to say. And then I feel wetness and know he is kissing me there. He stays there for a moment before he pulls away, and my wrists are freed.

"Get on the bed," he commands.

My phone starts ringing, but we both ignore it. He smirks as I climb onto the bed and spread my legs.

No point in hiding anything from him.

He's touched and played with more parts of me than my husband did in our ten years together.

And I like it.

A lot.

He hovers over me, coming between my legs, but my phone keeps on ringing.

"Get it," he demands. I crane my neck toward it, but I can't see a name.

"No."

"Get it," he repeats. His cock is at my entrance, teasing me as he pushes it in, then stops and does it again, not quite entering. "I'll let you have it if you answer your phone."

I reach for it and don't even look as I accept the call.

"Oriana," Kyler says.

I freeze, and Jake smiles. Then he slides in a little more, and I lick my lips while trying not to thrust my hips to meet his.

"Tell him you're on a date," Jake says.

"Oriana," Kyler calls my name again.

"I'm on a date," I say breathlessly, and Jake continues pushes in. My breathing snaps.

"Tell him you're enjoying it," Jake whispers.

"I'm enjoying it," I say, not even listening to what Kyler replies, my eyes fixated on Jake.

"Oriana, what are you doing?" Kyler asks.

"Tell him that you're at the sex club."

"I'm at the sex club."

"You're what," Kyler screams.

Jake pushes in a farther and croons, "That's my girl."

"Oh my God." I gasp as he goes in all the way, his finger rubbing my clit as I stretch around him. He feels so good, I can't think straight.

Reaching for my phone, he puts it to his ear as my hands find the bedding and squeeze.

"She's currently calling me God. I'd suggest you call back when she isn't." Then he hangs up.

I'm sure after this, I'll be mad.

But right now...

I'm in heaven.

CHAPTER 17
Not God, just Jake
JAKE

Having this redheaded beauty come undone on my cock is worth so much more than I knew possible.

I should be working. I'm always fucking working.

But this...*her*... Fuck!

It's like breathing in a cool winter breeze. It's fresh when it hits your lungs, and you know you have got to suck it in to get the full benefit.

She wiggles beneath me as I thrust in and out, her heels digging into my ass like the good girl she is, her phone discarded on the floor.

Who would have thought this beautiful angel on the bed could be so obedient when she's getting fucked.

I like it.

And I like *her*.

That's the real issue.

You should *not* like women you know belongs to someone else.

Because this woman does belong to someone else. The ring she still wears as I fuck her is a constant reminder. I wonder if she even realizes she still has it on or if it's simply a habit.

I'm not an adulterer, but she makes me one, and I don't care.

Her fingers spear into her hair and she clings to it as if she wants to tear it from her scalp. I lean forward and bite her tit, doing the same with the other so her memories of me will be scarred into her skin. I break the delicate flesh, but she doesn't care, she simply reaches for my hair as her hips meet mine, in and out and in and out.

Her cunt is my heaven, and I could spend years exploring her body and never tire of it.

That's an issue.

She is becoming an issue.

Taking up too much space in my head.

A place where she doesn't belong.

Luckily for her, her debt is now paid.

Our dates are done.

As is our time together.

"Jake." Her whimpering my name brings me back to the moment.

I lean down to her ear and breathe on her neck. "Yes?" I growl and bite her lobe. I can't help but bite her all over, that's the effect she has on me.

"Kiss me," she says.

I do, but not on her lips. I kiss her neck and suck, marking her for the fun of it, as she holds on like a koala bear.

Fucking her is my new favorite hobby.

Tasting her is like having the finest chocolate—I keep going back for more, even when I know I should stop.

"Oh my God!" She moans sensually, her body tensing around mine. I bite her shoulder as we both come in an explosion I won't soon forget. As she screams my name, her fingernails that were digging into my back relax. I wonder if she broke the skin? I guess I'll find out soon. I push into her again, unable to stop, and again, milking every moment with her while I can.

Oriana sinks into the bed, her hair a beautiful mess, breathing heavily, and her eyes, so green and vibrant, stare back at me with a smile.

"I've never come like that before," she confesses.

"Good."

"Jake?" she says, and I smile as I pull out of her and remove the condom.

"Yes?"

"Can we go again?"

I can't help the laugh that bubbles up. "You didn't think that was all, now, did you?" I raise a brow. "We still need you on your hands and knees."

Her jaw tics at my words before a wide smile blooms on her lips.

She stays where she is, lying there, being so perfect.

A knock comes on the door, and I know who it is before he even speaks.

"Company, boss."

She gets up slowly, covering herself with the blanket.

Standing, I dress quickly and when I look back, she hasn't moved.

"I think I should go," she says in a shy voice, so different from the woman just screaming and writhing beneath me.

"If you must." I shrug, turn for the door, and leave her there. Entering the main area of the club and spot Kier, Joey, and Lucas sitting at the bar. The club is almost completely empty as it's getting toward closing time, but the bartender stays behind, serving them drinks as they're part owners of the club.

I run everything, and everything is done through me, but in this town, you need protection, and that's exactly what these men are. Keir, the mafia boss, is not someone this city wants to mess with. He is ruthless, cunning, smart, and downright merciless, and so is his family. Joey, Keir's second in charge, is just as dangerous. And Lucas? He's known for the dirty work we all know he carries out for the Don.

"This is an unexpected visit," I comment as I step to the other side of the bar. "You can go. Close up and let yourself out," I direct the bartender.

He nods and takes his leave, while I finish making their drinks.

"Business brings us here," Keir states, taking the drink I put in front of him.

"I suspected so," I reply.

Joey looks at his phone and smiles—his new wife, I suspect. Lucas merely sits there quietly, looking around, not showing any emotion on his face.

"So, how can I help you?"

"A new player has entered the field. He's been asking around about this place."

My brows draw together. "And?"

Kier taps his fingers on the counter. "He owns clubs in LA, some in Vegas, and a few other cities. But he's looking to expand..." He pauses. "Here."

"What type of clubs?" I ask the question because if it was a normal bar, Keir wouldn't have an issue. There are other high-profile sex clubs in our area, but they aren't run as efficiently and effectively as this one. Keir knows of them all, and mine is the one that doesn't get fucked with, and the reason for that comes back to Keir.

"Playroom," he says, and I nod my head. I went to a playroom once. "We also heard you know him."

The door to the back area opens and Oriana steps out.

All eyes go to her.

Lucas leans on the counter and smiles, then looks at me and back to her. Keir just stares, unimpressed.

But it's Joey who speaks, "Kyler's wife?"

I grind my teeth at the mention of that asshole's name. Keir notices and studies me, but my eyes avert to Oriana, who's hugging herself, unsure what to do.

"Captain will take you home," I tell her.

"Were you just fucking?" Lucas asks with a smirk. "You can tell me."

She says nothing, just looks at me.

"Lucas," Joey warns.

Lucas throws up his hands and turns to me. "Didn't think you'd go for the good girls. I'm surprised, but how good is she if she's married?" Lucas says.

"Separated, actually," Oriana remarks, drawing our eyes to her once again. "I'll walk myself out, thanks." She strides past us on her way to the stairs.

"Oriana." She pauses, not looking back. "Captain will take you. Don't argue."

Captain nods and follows her out.

"You fucking the customers now?" Joey asks, and Keir and Lucas wait for me to answer. They know I don't fuck my girls or my customers.

It's a rule.

One I never break.

"No, she isn't a customer."

"The bogeyman..." I turn to Keir at the mention of his name, "is your brother, correct?"

I nod. There's no point denying it. Different mothers, same father. He's younger than me, not by much, and is well-known on the West Coast.

"We respect you, Jake. We have a mutual understanding and run a good business together. I do not extend that to visitors trying to upturn my town. If I were you, I would pass that information along to your brother before I do." Keir stands, Joey and Lucas follow, then they make for the exit. "One last thing. It's my wedding anniversary next weekend. You're coming. Bring a date."

"What if I have plans?" I say.

"Change them."

I smirk, and he nods his head before they leave.

A date.

This has me wondering if I can get Oriana to give me a third.

CHAPTER 18

New job, who dis?

ORIANA

O n my first day at the new job, my manager proceeded to give me a tour of the company. And when she showed me my desk, she asked about Kyler. *Of course*. I mean, I knew it was going to happen because it always does. People can't resist knowing everything there is to know about Kyler, after all, who doesn't love a rock star. I had hoped perhaps these questions would have come up later, once she got to know me a little more, but no! She asked if we were still together since he had been photographed kissing another woman.

Instantly, my mind went on alert. Not wanting to discuss anything to do with Kyler I answered with a simple "no" and gave nothing else.

Luckily, that was the end of that.

Because she didn't push and for that I was grateful.

As I'm only new and still learning, I don't have anything assigned to me all week. She mentioned it would probably stay that way for a few months until I can do everything with confidence and ease, so each day this week I have been shadowing other colleagues and their clients. Most of the stuff I do already know; I know how to be a personal assistant after years with Kyler. They interview all their candidates thoroughly and do full background checks on them as well. It's interesting to see how the other side works. Each assistant signs a non-disclosure agreement, and if they breach it, the consequences are steep. But most are just excited to work for someone famous.

I want to tell them it isn't all it's cracked up to be, but I don't and keep my opinions to myself.

On Friday, as I am leaving the office, I see Jake leaning against my new car. It's a small Toyota, nothing as flashy like I used to drive, but it is more affordable. His Porsche sits behind my car, blocking me in. I pause halfway between the office and the parking lot, my heart already speeding up at the sight of him and my mind switching into overdrive about what he might want.

I haven't heard from Jake all week, not since I left his club that night and Captain dropped me off at home without a word. I know he has my number, and I guess I have his, but I wasn't sure what to say.

Thanks for rocking my world. No.

Kyler, on the other hand, has been calling and messaging non-stop. It's at the point where I'm almost ready to change my number so I don't have to deal with him.

"Do you plan to take a few more steps over here to talk?" Jake asks.

Goddamn, I've become frozen to the spot and can't seem to move, so I simply say, "That depends. Why are you here?"

"I need a favor."

"A favor?" My face scrunches in confusion. *What could this man possibly need from me?*

"Yes. I need someone to assist me at a work function."

"Like a date?"

His lip quirks with a devilish smirk. "No. Our dates aren't dates. They are fucking. I'm not opposed to fucking you, Oriana, but this *is* about business."

"So, it's business?" My eyes narrow, now intrigued.

"Yes."

"What do I get out of it?" I take a step closer.

He pushes off the car, that smirk never leaving his face. "I'll fuck you in the car after." He leans in close to my ear. "Have you ever been fucked in a Porsche, Oriana?"

"No," I say breathlessly. He knows I come from

money, but the way he says it makes me believe he knows my sex life has been very vanilla, and having sex with someone in a car...well, that sounds like fun.

"Good. I'll pick you up tomorrow." Jake turns, gets in his car, and drives off.

I stay where I am, thoughts whirling, wondering why I agreed to his demand.

Did I even actually agree?

HARVEY IS AWAY AGAIN, so when a knock comes on his door while I'm getting ready, I know it's not for him. Sucking in a breath, I tell myself I should ignore it. Right?

I tighten the towel around me when the knock comes again. My hair and makeup are done and I am all but ready except for the dress, which I am struggling with.

"Who is it?"

"Are you expecting someone else?" I freeze at my husband's voice. "Oriana." Why, when he says my name now, does it annoy me? "I know you can hear me."

"I can," I confirm. "I'm busy. I have plans."

"This can't wait."

"I'm sure it can," I say, still not opening the door.

"*Oriana*." Releasing a breath, I open the door slowly. His eyes find mine and then instantly look me up and down.

"What's so important it can't wait?" I ask.

As he steps in without invitation, I step back, my hand still on the door. Kyler walks into my brother's place like he has been here hundreds of times. He hasn't because he hated visiting family and especially mine.

"Do you have a date?" he asks.

I pull the towel even tighter, huffing, not wanting to answer his questions

"Do you?" I fire back at him. "Pamela, wasn't it?" I refer to the woman he kissed in the picture that's splashed on every magazine front page. "How is she?"

I met her once. Pamela's a model, and she is absolutely beautiful. If I could put two women next to one another and call them opposites, it would be the two of us.

"That was just for press," he says, not so convincingly.

"I'm sure it was."

"Can you say the same? Can you say you are seeing Jake for pictures in a magazine?" He steps closer to where I stand, still holding the door open.

"You should leave. I have to get ready."

"For a date?"

"Yes, actually."

That voice—it instantly has my stomach flipping.

We both turn to see Jake standing on the front stoop. He is dressed in blue slacks and a white button-up shirt with a couple of buttons undone at the top, and his sleeves rolled up.

"We have a date...." Jake's eyes lock on me, "and you aren't dressed."

I nod, my body warming as his gaze travels the length of me.

"We were talking," Kyler says. "You have some nerve. You know that, right?"

"Do I?" Jake asks incredibly casually. "It was you who let her walk away. Or am I mistaken?" Jake's eyes flick to mine.

"You were my friend," Kyler says angrily.

"Correction, Kyler, we were acquainted."

"You were at our wedding."

My eyes go wide at that statement.

He was?

How did I not know this?

How could I have missed that?

Our wedding was a massive spectacle. Elaborate—the word is not sufficient to describe the type of event we had solely put on for the cameras. I didn't plan a single part of it, but at the time I was simply happy to be there because above all, I loved him.

"You were at my wedding?" I ask Jake.

Kyler huffs from the side, but I can't concentrate on him and his bullshit. Instead, my eyes zero in on Jake.

"You should get changed. We'll be late."

"You never said anything," I say to him, why wouldn't be he say something to me, looking back at my husband. "It's time you leave, Kyler."

Kyler's feet stay stuck to the ground, his mouth opens and closes as if he can't believe what I just said.

"How dare you pick him over me, Oriana. We need to talk."

I roll my eyes. "Please...go talk to Pamela. I don't have time to listen to you or your excuses." I wave toward the door where Jake is still standing. "You can leave now."

Kyler looks between us both as he steps closer. "He isn't who he says he is. Remember that." I nod because that's all I can give him as he storms out.

Jake steps in, completely unbothered by all the drama, and I shut the door behind him.

"He wants you back for the sole reason he can no longer have you." Jake's words hit me hard, and I know they're true. But it doesn't make the sting of them any less painful.

"I'll get dressed," I say, turning for my bedroom with a slight huff.

"I'll help."

I stop as I reach my door. "No need, I can get dressed by myself."

"I'm sure you can, but I'd rather assist in the matter." He gives me a grin that would melt my panties if I were wearing any.

Stepping into my room, I go to the three outfits I have on the bed and look back at him. I was unsure what type of event we were going to, so I laid out a few options to choose from.

He walks up, points to the one with the leather skirt, and says, "This one."

"The event's not dressy?" I ask.

"It's an anniversary party. I was invited for the sole reason his wife wants people other than just their family there."

"So, these are your friends?" I ask, curious. We don't really talk about personal things, and for all I know, the stories of Jake tied to the mafia could be true.

"We work together."

"Oh, okay." I nod and reach for the outfit he picked, and he sits on the edge of my bed, watching me.

"You can get changed here. It's not like I haven't seen and tasted almost every inch of you."

I smile at his words and look away before I drop

the towel then slide my panties on, followed by a low-cut bra. When I glance back at him, his eyes are on me, locked and loaded.

"We could be late," he husks.

"Late?"

Jake stands, backs me up to the wall, and is flush against my body before I can even blink.

It's then I realize that Jake has never kissed me.

He has kissed and licked everywhere but my lips.

"What are you doing?" I ask with a gasp.

"Shh." He leans forward, his mouth molding to my shoulder, his teeth digging in. Jake's hand slowly crawls down my belly until it breaches my panties, and he dips in a finger, making me suck in a deep breath. "I think dessert should be had before the main course, wouldn't you agree?"

I nod eagerly. *How can I not?*

"What's your favorite dessert?" I ask.

His eyes find mine, and the playfulness sparkling in them is intoxicating.

"You," he replies before he drops to his knees in front of me and removes my panties with his teeth while his hand continues to toy with me.

When my panties reach my knees, he moves in, his fingers halting, and kisses me where my slit starts. He does it once, twice, three times before he slides his tongue up to my clit and sucks. I yelp in surprise and grab onto him. Chuckling, he continues his torture, the sensation pushing me toward that wonderful feeling. My head falls back and hits the wall as his mouth works overtime, making me come in what seems like only a minute.

I have never come so hard and fast in my life.

Just a few licks, fingers inside pumping nice and fast, and I am putty in his hands.

How have I missed out on this my whole life?

The problem is, now it's all I want.

All I dream about.

When he's done, he stands, pulls up my panties, and leans into my ear. "Get dressed. We're late." Pressing a kiss to my neck, he steps back, leaving me breathless as I manage to dress and make myself decent somehow. I'm buzzing from head to toe with every move I make.

He watches the whole time until I slide on a pair of heels. When I reach for my bag, he shakes his head.

"You won't need it."

"My phone," I say.

"You won't need that either." I want to argue with him, but I don't. Instead, I listen and follow him out. Once I lock the door behind me, he takes the keys and slides them into his pocket as we make our way to his Porsche. He opens the door, letting me in before he goes to the driver's side.

"Your driver not with you tonight?"

"He wasn't invited."

"I thought he went everywhere you went."

"Not tonight." He starts the car and pulls out.

"Where is it that we are going?"

"An anniversary party."

"I got that. Do you know them well?"

His fingers drum on the steering wheel before he says, "You could say that."

"Okaaay." It's all I can think to say.

He smirks but says nothing more as we continue to drive. His phone rings and he mutes it, ignoring the call before he comes to a stop outside a brownstone. The house is marvelous—actually, that word doesn't describe it well enough, it's incredible. I personally think all brownstones are amazing, as they have that older vibe yet modern feel to them.

Someone opens Jake's door. "Sir, I'll park for you."

Jake gets out and comes around to my side, opening my door and taking my hand as I slide out of the vehicle.

"Are you sure what I'm wearing is okay? They have valet," I ask, concern now etching in my voice.

He looks me over again. I'm dressed in a leather skirt, a long-sleeved man's shirt that is cut off and buttoned up the front, with a bulky necklace and heels to match.

"Stunning," he answers, his gaze burning with lust. I blush at his single descriptive word, and his hand cups my cheek as he strokes it with his thumb before he says.

"It's the same color as your pussy lips." I'm sure my face goes redder at his vulgar comment. "Did you like how I didn't use *that* word?" he asks, then leans in and whispers in my ear not being able to resist, "Yours is my favorite cunt."

"Jake!" I breathe out, trying to scold, when really, my voice is nothing but an aroused whisper. Seeing right through me, he laughs, pulling away and walking up the stairs.

"I tell no lies, Oriana," he says as the door opens.

When it does, all three men from the other night at the club are standing there. The one near the stairs holds a blonde woman close to his side while the other two are in conversation. A man greets and welcomes us in.

I look to Jake, who nods his head at the first two.

"Lucas, Joey, this is Oriana." Both men turn to face us, and I grip hard onto Jake, not wanting him to let go. I'm used to being on someone's arm during parties —it's all I have ever done, but this party is full of men who are truly scary.

"The one you are fucking, correct?" the man, who I am guessing is Lucas, questions. He is dressed in a suit, much like the others, but his suit appears far more expensive. There's an air about him that screams danger.

The other man offers me a kind smile, and even though he is covered in tattoos doesn't give off quite the same air of danger as Lucas. Don't get me wrong, he is still unnerving.

"Yes, the very one," Jake replies.

"And she's married to the rock star. Tell me, how is your husband doing?"

"Lucas, leave the woman alone," Joey says. "Do you not have your girlfriend here to annoy?"

"You are my favorite person to annoy, you already know this." Lucas smiles at Joey, and when he does, a chill runs down my spine before he looks back at me. "You don't know who we are, do you?"

"Should I?" I ask, confused.

They all smirk as a few women walk out and begin to introduce themselves.

CHAPTER 19

Mafia who?

JAKE

Keir is married to Sailor, who just so happens to be the nicest woman I have ever met. She has to be to put up with Keir. Keir's brother, Joey, is married to Adora, who owns a small bookstore he bought for her. I know Adora the best out of all the women, thanks to our time in Italy together, when I brought her back to Joey. And Chanel, who is a flight attendant, is with Lucas, the craziest one of the lot. And then we have Piper, who is a badass bitch. All four of them usually go everywhere together, and their women are close-knit. Sailor starts talking to Oriana as she stays glued to my side, her hand in mine, not letting go.

"I can steal you away, can't I? This is the most people Keir has invited into our home, and I'm so excited to make new friends and learn all about the rock star life," she says to Oriana, who tenses. Sailor must notice because she adds, "I mean, what life was like for you, *not him*." She brushes it off, and Oriana looks at me.

I know all eyes are on us.

"I'll be back," she says.

I lean down and whisper in her ear, "Don't go far. The front seat of a Porsche is waiting for us." Her cheeks go crimson before she looks down and follows Sailor.

"She has no idea who we are?" Lucas says, laughing as she steps away. "I like it. How on earth could she *not* know?" He shakes his head, still laughing. "Even that dipshit of a husband knows."

"Do you plan to keep her?" Keir asks.

"No." Their gazes all fix on me as Joey offers me a drink. I take it as I glance around. There's Keir's mother and Lucas's mother in the other room, and they are entertaining all the kids.

"So quick to answer." Lucas whistles.

"Your brother is shopping around," Keir adds. "It's making me anxious. If I were you, I would warn him I don't like people sticking their noses where they're not wanted. And that's the only warning I will give."

I haven't seen or heard from my brother for over ten years.

Keir's name is called, and Sailor walks in.

"Come, everything's ready out back." Keir takes her hand and leads the way, and we all follow to the outdoor area, which is glowing with fairy lights, a small bar, a table full of food, and soft music playing. I spot Oriana straight away, talking to Adora. She smiles at something Adora says before she looks up and catches me staring at her.

I'm not going to lie. My plan has been, and always will be, to just fuck her. I mean, look at her. Who the fuck wouldn't? Her husband's loss, letting someone like Oriana walk out of his life, only to realize too late what he lost and try to get her back.

I watch as she finishes her conversation with Adora, excuses herself, then makes her way toward me. Her long legs eat up the distance between us, the curves of her body hypnotizing me with every step she takes. When she comes to a stop in front of me, she tilts her face up and smiles, and I hate that I like it so much.

"These are your friends?" she asks, looking over her shoulder.

"Not really," I answer.

"Jake, Jake, Jake... That hurt, right in the heart," Joey jokes as he walks past us. He winks at Oriana as he continues on.

"Kind of," I amend.

"Thank you for inviting me."

I slide my hands into my pockets to keep from touching her. "I had to bring a date, and since our time got cut short last time..."

"Yeah." She pushes her hair behind her ear, and her voice drops down to a whisper as she says, "Casual sex. Is that what we are?"

"Do you wish to discuss this here?" She glances over her shoulder before looking back at me.

"I guess not." She shrugs, her lips pursed. "I like the women. They all seem nice."

"They are, despite their partners."

"I can still hear you," Joey yells. "Oriana, why don't you come over here and tell us how you met our Jake."

Raising a brow, I shake my head at him, then give Oriana a slight nod and walk over with her. Lucas has Chanel on his lap, and his hand strokes her shoulder. Keir is being forced to dance with Sailor, which is quite funny, considering he is just standing there with his hands on her hips as she sways.

"Take a seat," Lucas says, pointing to a chair. Oriana hesitates a moment, then does just that. Chanel leans over and hands her a drink,

"How Jake and I met..." Oriana starts, turning her head and finding my eyes as I stand behind her. I say nothing as she looks back to Joey. "He saved me one night. I didn't really know who he was then, but I saw him again at a gala, and well, here we are," she says simply.

"How many times have you two fucked?" Lucas asks, and Chanel hits his arm, while looking at Oriana apologetically.

"Lucas isn't used to guests. Ignore him. You don't have to answer him," Chanel tells her.

"Oral or intercourse?" Oriana asks him without missing a beat, surprising all of us.

Lucas raises a brow, and everyone goes silent as I lay my hand on her shoulder.

"We may not kill you yet, redhead." Lucas smiles.

I feel Oriana's shoulder tense at Lucas's words.

But then she relaxes at my touch.

CHAPTER 20

Fuck in the car?

ORIANA

"Oriana." I turn back to look at Sailor, who's standing with Keir by her side. His eyes are solely on her, and I wonder if my husband ever looked at me that way.

I doubt it.

Actually, no I don't doubt it, I know he never once looked at me the way Keir is looking at Sailor right now.

"Yes?" I answer.

"I hope to see you again. We don't see enough of Jake as it is. He's always so busy. Thank you both for coming." She smiles and hugs me.

Jake and I are the last two left. Keir and Jake got to talking, and Sailor was showing me her shoe collection, which, I might add, is out of this world. She gushed over every single pair as if they were her children.

"Happy anniversary," I tell them as Jake places his hand on my hip and leads me outside.

When we get to his car, the valet hands Jake his key, then he unlocks the car and holds the door open for me. I climb in and watch as he walks around to the driver's side and slides in. Jake starts the car, his hand tight on the steering wheel as he drives. He hits the highway and looks over at me.

"Would you like to come to mine for a drink?" I ask. I've never invited another man into my home before, never mind one that I intend to sleep with.

This is all so new to me.

All so exciting.

"You don't want to fuck in the car?" Jake asks, taking the exit to my place.

I bite my lip. "There isn't much room," I reply, scanning the car's interior. I have a feeling the steering wheel would be on my ass.

"You only need to bounce on my cock, Oriana."

Gosh! I blush at his words, something I cannot seem to stop doing around him.

Facing the window, I touch cheeks to try to cool them down. He reaches for my hand and pulls it to him, straight to his crotch. I feel how hard he is through his pants. Jake smirks when I grip it, and he puts both hands on the wheel, leaving my hand there.

"I wanted you the minute I tasted you. My cock is

rock hard thinking about what it's going to be like sliding into that pussy again." The way he speaks to me has me dizzy with want. I need him inside me. Right. This. Second.

I pull my hand away, reach under my skirt, and slide my panties off. Then I unbutton my shirt, my core tightening when he turns into the street, and we're almost there. He slows down and comes to a stop out the front of my place, puts the car in park, and slides the seat back, all in one smooth but equally heady movement.

Tapping his leg, his eyes lock on mine. "Come and get it," he tells me, licking his lip as his eyes drift to my chest. I do as he says and climb over him as gracefully as I can. My knees land on either side of his hips, and the steering wheel digs into my back as I hover right there.

Jake pushes the hair away from my face and softly says, "You can have full control."

"Full control?" I ask, shocked and a little intimidated.

He nods, and I look down between us.

"Get your tits out, please." My red lacy bra peeks out from between the two halves of the shirt. I pull it open and look back at him. As much as I loved hearing him say please, I reply, "I think I would prefer to keep the bra on." I'm exposed enough as it is, straddling him in his car, in full view of anyone walking by.

"Okay," he relents, and I feel his cock twitch between my legs. I manage to slip my hand between us to unzip his pants. I do it slow and deliberate, and he silently watches me, keeping his hands to himself the whole time.

"So, you don't plan to touch me?" I ask as I reach in and pull his hard cock free. I run my thumb over the tip feeling his piercing, and he sucks in a breath.

"No, it's all you."

"Full control," I repeat.

"Full," he whispers.

I do as he says, taking full control, and position him where I want him. He groans when the head of his cock meets my wet center, but he doesn't move. Neither of us does. It's like the air in the car has been sucked out and all I can hear is my heart beating rapidly in my ears.

"You should sit," he says, grinding his teeth.

I smile at the power he has given me, so I lean forward to touch my lips to his, but he moves so my lips press against his cheek. "Sit," he says into my ear, the sound filled with needy want.

Brushing my lips down his neck, I lean into his ear and say, "But it feels so good," as I rub against him, teasing him a bit more. I smirk as I feel him tense, another husky groan vibrating against me.

"Fuck, you make me insane." He growls and it's so insanely manly it almost makes me come on the spot.

"Good." I press down a little farther until I can feel him just barely enter me. "Do I still have full control?" I ask, biting his ear.

"Always," he replies, and my heart swells that this man gives me, someone he barely knows full control. It is a gift. One I've never had before.

A knock comes on the window as I lower myself down, and we both moan loudly as I sink on him. I hide my face in his chest, and his arms come around me.

"What?" he barks, his hands gripping my hips.

"Tell my wife to get out of your car."

Oh shit! I freeze at that voice.

"No can do. You see, I'm currently deep inside of her... A place you once visited and then abandoned," Jake says smugly.

"Jake!" I groan into his chest. He pushes his hips up, and I bite him through his shirt to stop a yelp from leaving me.

Kyler bangs on the window from outside, and Jake just laughs.

"Can you not see I'm busy, Kyler," Jake taunts as he pushes his hips up again, deeper this time. I stay hidden in his chest but can't stop the whimper that escapes. "It's best you go away, so I can finish fucking your wife and showing her how to come. Showing her what a real man is capable of."

"Oh my God, you did not just say that." I push off him, and when I do, I pin my eyes on Kyler. "Leave. Can you just *leave*?" I shout at him. "I can't move if you stay standing there watching."

"Why not? Maybe he likes to watch his wife get fucked. Since he never seemed to do it right himself." The glass smashes, and I scream, falling back into Jake's chest as he wraps his arms around me.

"Get the fuck out of the car," Kyler seethes.

Jake pushes me up until we're eye-to-eye.

"I need you to climb back into your seat but be extremely careful when you do it." Nodding, I lift off him and do as he says.

Jake wipes the glass away so I can climb over without hurting myself. As soon as I'm back in the passenger seat, I pull my skirt down, open the door, and get out of the car, my whole body trembling.

Turning around, I see Kyler standing there, hands clenched at his sides. Jake climbs out of the car, and as soon as his feet are on the ground, his hands go straight to Kyler's throat. He walks him backward until they reach the building across the street, and he slams Kyler into it. I hear Jake snarl, and I freeze on the spot.

"If you ever, *ever...* do anything as stupid as that again to hurt Oriana, I'll slice you from your neck to your dick and watch you bleed out like the pig you are. Do. You. Fucking. Hear. Me?"

I swallow hard at the protectiveness in his voice. Even with the nerves rushing through me, he makes me feel safe.

"What do you care what happens to her? You're only using her to fuck her," Kyler bites back, his voice harsh and low from the hand around his throat. Jake squeezes tighter, applying more pressure.

"Jake." I try to get his attention.

Kyler and I have issues, but I don't want him hurt. That is the last thing I want.

"Do you even know who this man is, Oriana?" Kyler rasps through Jake's tightening grip.

"She knows all she needs to know," Jake says.

And instantly I wonder what that means.

"Jake, let him go." After a moment, Jake does as I say and steps back, then he reaches for me and looks back to Kyler. "You only want her because someone else has her," Jake accuses.

"Is that what this is? You having her?" Kyler scoffs.

"Well, from what I remember, you saw me inside of her, did you not?" Jake bites back.

"Can this night just end already?" I groan. Both men focus on me, and I can't help the agitated tone that leaves me. "Kyler, go home. I don't even know why you're here. *Again*."

"I've been waiting for you all night. And then I couldn't believe what I saw when you pulled up. I sat there, stunned, not sure it was you." His expression goes from shocked to pleading as he continues, "This is what you wanted, right? For me to see you? I have seen, and it's time you come home."

Jake starts laughing. I glare at him, but Kyler doesn't take his eyes off me.

"And you pick someone who is a known ally of the mafia. Do you know how that looks," Kyler yells.

"I..."

"Mafia, Oriana. Do you understand what mafia is?" Kyler almost yells the last words.

"How would you know any of this?" I ask.

Kyler looks to Jake, who's standing silently next to me.

"Everyone in this city knows who they are, who *he* is. Jake is in their back pocket. For God's sake open your eyes, Oriana. He owns businesses with them."

Jake grunts.

We both turn to him.

"I'm in no one's back pocket. At least get your facts right."

"Which part did I get wrong? Tell me? Tell her it's the mafia..." Kyler smiles like he knows he has won something, "because you know you can't deny it."

"Well, your sweet wife here just dined with them," he replies, then he addresses me, "How bad would you say they were?"

What does he mean? Oh, sugar, how could I have not known that?

"You had dinner with the mafia, Oriana? What on earth are you doing?" Kyler asks incredulously.

"Jake, we need to go." I pull him away from Kyler and straight to the front door. Unlocking and opening it, I push him inside and shut the door behind us. Turning the lock, I spin to face him. "Did you just take me to a mafia house?" I screech.

"I took you to Keir and Sailor's house, yes," he says, smiling. "If I remember correctly, you enjoyed yourself."

"I did, but why would you take me there?"

He shrugs. "I needed a date, and you seemed to be the right choice."

"I think you should leave." I pull my shirt tighter and my skirt down further, feeling somewhat awkward and uneasy.

"Why? Do I make you uncomfortable now?"

I start twirling my hair nervously and look at the door. "Please l-leave," I say firmly, though my voice cracks.

Jake nods and, without another word, walks out, closing the door behind him. I follow and lock it. Going to my room, I shut that door and fall onto my bed.

What have I gotten myself into?

CHAPTER 21

Time for you to leave

"Your little girlfriend is here," Captain says as he knocks on the door.

I turn to look at the screens and see Oriana, dressed in jeans and jacket, walking down the stairs and heads straight to the bar.

"And she's asking for you."

Oriana has been a ghost for the last few weeks, and I have been too busy to chase her.

"Tell her to leave," I say.

He raises a brow. "Are you sure?"

"Yes. Now, get her the fuck out of here."

Captain nods and walks off. I watch on the screen as he goes up to her at the bar and says something. She shakes her head and looks up at the camera, and then she flips me the finger.

I can't help but laugh.

She's angry.

Really furious.

My innocent girl gave me the finger.

I want to stab myself for calling her *my girl*.

Captain leaves her at the bar, and I see him heading back this way. He knocks and then opens the door. "She told me to tell you to stop watching her and get out there and talk to her like a real man." He pauses, then adds, "I like her," before he ducks off.

I remain where I am, watching her on the screen. The bartender gives her a glass of water, and she thanks him as she looks to the door, then back at the camera. She sits there staring—at me—as I contemplate if I should go out there or not.

Decision made, I head out to the main area.

As soon as the door opens, her laughter fills my ears before it's cut short when her eyes find mine. As I approach, the bartender moves to the other end of the counter while I pull the stool out next to her and sit.

"No one is allowed in here unless they are wearing a wristband." I look at her wrists and don't see one.

"The girl at the door tried to give me one, but I ignored her." She shrugs. "You don't call? Text?" she asks.

"Why would I do either? We were only fucking. I

had no use for you this week. And you told me to leave the last time I saw you, so I figured we were done."

Her hand lifts and touches a lock of her red hair. "You took me to..." she leans in to whisper the rest, "a mafia house." She pulls back, her eyes wide, expecting me to react.

"I can take you to a lot worse than that," I tell her.

Captain comes up behind us, taps my shoulder to get my attention, then I turn back to her. "You shouldn't have come tonight. I have meetings." I stand from the stool when I see my brother walk into the club. We are the same height but differ in every other way. He is dressed as if he works in a morgue, whereas I am dressed for business. He smiles when he sees me—

a smile so goddamn bright it could be blinding.

He hates to smile.

So I know he's only doing it to piss me off.

"Brother," he greets as he steps closer and offers me his hand. I don't take it. That's when he notices Oriana. His eyes trace her up and down before they stop on her face. She offers one of her kind smiles, and I grind my teeth and say nothing.

"We can take this to my office."

My brother scans the place with narrowed eyes. "This is..." he flicks his gaze to Oriana, "cute." Then his eyes come back to me. "But we know you can do better. I mean, I've done better," he says. "You need to visit my playrooms, brother. I think you'll be pleasantly surprised."

When I say nothing, he turns back to Oriana again and his obvious interest is infuriating. "Do you work for Jake?" he asks, and she shakes her head. "So, a customer?" She shakes her head again. "Interesting." He looks at me. "Very interesting."

Then he's smiling wider. "The Jake I know doesn't do the same woman for long. Is she due to be traded in? If so, I would like a turn." He turns back to her, his gaze traveling down her body. "I have a thing for redheads."

Oriana stands from the stool, takes a step back, and meets my eyes. "It's best you don't call me. I made a mistake," she states with a little more distaste in her voice as her hand goes to her hip.

I nod at Captain, and he guides Oriana out as I focus back on my brother. "What the fuck are you planning?" I ask.

He steps up to the bar, taps it, and nods to the whiskey before he answers, "I came to see my brother."

"No, you didn't. You came to shop."

He shrugs, taking the drink that's put in front of him. "And that."

"You need to leave. Go back to where you came

from. You are making a lot of people unhappy in this town," I tell him.

"Oh, so they know I'm here. I guess they are as good as their reputation..." He pauses. "And in your pocket too?"

"No. Just business."

He nods his head. "My intention wasn't to come here to stir shit up. I came to see you."

"Me? Since when have you ever chosen to come to see me?" I question.

"Women don't want to work. They just want the money. And I heard you have a special way of getting women and keeping them loyal to you."

"You came for information," I say, and he nods.

"And, of course, to see you. What has it been...ten years, brother?" He pauses, swirling the liquor in his glass. "And to warn you... If you shop for women again in my sites, the hunters may just very well kill you, and no mafia will be able to stop them."

The hunters are three brothers—if they even are brothers, that is—who do exactly as their title describes, they hunt. And they are known for always getting it right with a one hundred percent kill rate. Keir was going to hire them, but his connections outreached them. So he used his own. I didn't realize he was connected to them.

"Warning received. You can leave now that you've seen me."

"Maybe I might stay in town. It's been a while." Grayson smiles as he heads out the same way he came in. "I'll drop by tomorrow, brother. I know where you live."

CHAPTER 22

"Drugs are bad, kids!"

ORIANA

M y job is great.

After the first week, people got over the fact I was married to Kyler and now talk to me about me. It's nice not to have to speak about Kyler all the time, considering most of my adult life has been about him and it's tiring.

I signed the divorce papers and sent them in this week. He may not be happy about it, but it's time to move on. I have to move on.

Jake helped me with that, and I was hoping to see him and thank him that night I went back to the club. But it was clear he didn't want anything to do with me, and taking me to that house with those mafia people? Well, I don't even know how to feel about that.

I liked them, but now knowing who they are, I'm not sure I want to see them anywhere again.

As I walk out to my car, Callie tells me about her plans for the holidays. She is going to Bali with her husband for their ten-year wedding anniversary. She shows me the new ring he got her, and I smile. It's simple, with a lovely diamond in the middle.

Kyler insisted I wear the biggest ring. It annoyed me, all the time continuously rolling around when I typed. Something like Callie is wearing is perfect.

"Do you have plans?" she asks as she opens her car door and throws her bag inside. "Also, who is that fine specimen leaning on your car?" I spin around and see Jake's brother standing there. How did I not see him when I walked out?

"That's—"

"A fine piece of man, that's for sure," she whispers. "Do you have these men stored somewhere?"

"I should go. Have a good holiday."

"Have a good night." She leans in and kisses my cheek before I turn in the direction of my car. He's standing there, watching me in a way that makes me uneasy. Sucking in a breath, I slowly make my way across the lot. He's blocking my car door, so I can't get in, and he makes no move to shift out of the way when I approach.

"You really don't work for him," are the first words out of his mouth.

"I don't," I confirm.

"Interesting," he says, crossing his arms over his chest. I can see the similarities between the two. Both are around the same height, with strong jaws and full lips, but the eyes are where they differ. They're so different.

"I'm Oriana." I offer my hand. His eyes flick to it, and he licks his lips before he takes it. "You already knew that, though, didn't you?"

He holds on to my hand.

"I did. It's curious... I never really took my brother for the redhead type."

"I never took him to have a brother who specializes in stalking," I bite back.

He clicks his tongue. "And she has fire." He drops my hand and steps away from my car, so I can open the door. "Care to accompany me for dinner?"

"That's a hard no." I smile to lessen the blow. "I don't even know your name."

"Grayson," he says. "But those who know me call me the bogeyman."

I try to stop the laugh that bubbles up, but I can't. I cover my mouth with my hand and laugh into it.

"You do know *who* you have been fucking, right? You seem...sweet. Innocent. I wonder if that was the attraction."

"It possibly was, but what does it matter to you?" I ask, lifting a brow.

"I'm telling you right now you aren't aware who you are lying with. Jake hasn't gotten where he is today by being a good boy. Do you know I learned from him? And when I realized he was happy and content where he was, but I wanted more, I left. And I made myself bigger, scarier. Do you want to know why they call me the bogeyman?" he asks, leaning down into my personal space. "It's because I have no problem killing you when you sleep. And when those eyes open as I slice your throat, I'm the last person you will see." He pushes away. "Bogeyman." He smirks. "I'll be seeing you, Oriana."

"Goodbye, Grayson," I say as calmly as possible, holding back the scream I want let rip as I watch him leave. As soon as he's gone, I get into my car and lock the doors, calling Jake with trembling fingers.

He answers straight away.

"Let's get one thing straight. We are *not* an item. You need to stop introducing me to killers, and y-you..." I pause, trying to rein in my shaking voice. "You need to stay out of my life. And your brother too. Both of you," I blurt before he can even say hello.

"You've seen my brother?" he asks apprehensively.

"Yes. I'm watching him get into his car as we speak. He was outside of my work, waiting for me by my car."

"I'll handle it," he assures.

"Good. And lose my number. I never want to see

you again." I hang up on him, start the car, and drive straight home. As soon as I'm inside, I lock the door and open a bottle of wine.

How has my life gone from being married.

To separated.

To having the best sex of my life.

To now...

What-the-fuck-is-happening?

Right now I plan to drown myself in a bottle of wine, waiting for my best friend to come over with pizza.

I may be drunk when she arrives if she doesn't get here soon. I pour a glass, and drink it down quickly, followed by a second before a knock comes on the door, and I hear Simone's voice on the other side. Gripping the bottle—because I decided to give up on the glass—I throw the door open. She holds two boxes of pizzas and has a huge smile on her lips.

"I brought us brownies..." She laughs. "Special brownies." She holds the bag up, shaking it. "We need to eat one before the pizza." She puts everything on the counter, removes the bottle of wine from my grip, and hands me a brownie. I eat it without a second thought before she opens the pizza. "Dig in." She takes out her own brownie and sits opposite me. "So, Kyler was on your front steps. I told him to fuck off."

I groan and drop my head into my hands.

"He had papers in his hand. I'm guessing divorce papers?" she asks, as I told her I sent them to him.

"Yep, needed to be done," I say, reaching for the bottle of wine. "I've been having great sex with someone who is a possible killer." I groan. "How does one deal with that?"

"Hold up, you what?" she asks, mouth agape.

I start to feel lightheaded and lie down on the floor, the cold tiles soothing my skin.

"I think I'm drunk."

"Or baked." Simone laughs.

"Baked?" I ask, confused, not moving.

"Yes, those brownies have a *little something extra* in them."

"Oh gosh. Not only am I drunk, I'm stoned. And had sex with a serial killer. I should add this to my resume, get street cred..." I whine as I feel Simone sit on the floor next to me. She brings the pizza with her, though. "And I made friends with mafia wives." I clap my hands, and the sarcastic look? I have that mastered right now. "Yay me."

"Come on, think about it like this... You have gotten life experience. Before, you would have dressed up for a gala or event and that's it. Stayed by Kyler's side and talked to who he wanted you to talk to." She shrugs. "It's good, isn't it?"

"Oriana." I close my eyes as I hear my name.

"I'm pretty high, I th...think," I slur, my eyes still closed. "Because I can hear my mother saying my name."

"Yeah, I think its because she's at the door." I fly into a seated position, banging heads with Simone, cracking my nose on her forehead.

"Fuck!" she shouts. "That hurt."

"Sorry." I look to the door, holding my nose. "Are we just high?" I whisper.

But soon after a knock follows, and I groan as I hear my mother's voice again. "Pretend we aren't here. We can hide." I get on my hands and knees and go to hide behind the couch when my mother's voice filters through the door, "I can hear you, Oriana." She sounds annoyed.

"Sugar," I fake-swear. I look back to see Simone, still on the floor, eating her pizza. Managing to stand, I walk to the door and reluctantly pull it open. My mother stands there with a large bag in her hand, and a whole pile of disappointment written all over her face.

"You haven't called."

"I've been busy," I tell her.

Mother walks in and wraps her arms around me, dropping her bag as she hugs me. "So I've heard. It's why I came to see you." She hugs me tighter before she lets me go and pulls away. "I see you both are still

169

causing trouble," she says, looking to Simone, who hasn't moved from the floor.

"Sorry, Mrs. Lavender."

I help Simone up as my mother walks into the kitchen and opens the other pizza box, pulling out a slice and eating it quite quickly.

"What's the plans?" Her eyes fall on me. "Kyler rang me."

I groan.

How can a man be so distant in a relationship and then, after, be more available than ever? It literally makes no sense. I look to Simone for help, but she goes to the sitting area and flicks on the television totally ignoring me. Typical, when the going gets tough...

When I turn back, my mother has half a brownie in her mouth.

Oh hell...

"You shouldn't eat that," I warn.

"Why? It's amazing. You did good. You must give me the recipe."

Simone starts laughing, hard, falling to the couch until we can't see her anymore but we can still hear her.

"You didn't bake it?" my mother asks, nodding to where Simone is roaring with laughter.

"Mom, that has marijuana baked into it." I watch the horror cross my mother's face. Her eyes go wide, and she throws the brownie, glaring at it before she picks up the closest drink, which just so happens to be my wine, and chugs it all.

"You let me eat it," she accuses.

"Technically, you didn't ask. You just ate it." I shrug. "I ate one, and I'm still alive." I sit back on the floor and lie down again. "I feel just a little tired, like I'm falling through the floor. That's all I feel."

Simone keeps on laughing.

My mother gasps as if realization has dawned about something. "Does this make me a druggie? I've never had drugs. Oh gosh, what if I become addicted?"

Simone loses it. She is in hysterics.

"I'm sure you won't," I tell her at the same time Simone yells between her hysterics, "Drugs are bad, kids, you get addicted."

It's the same wording my mother used to say to us as children.

"Simone," my mother yells. Holding the bottle of wine, she lies down next to me. "The floor is nice and cold."

"It is," I agree.

"And my daughter is getting divorced," Mom says.

"I am," I whisper.

"Are you happy?"

"Right now, she is," Simone yells.

I laugh at her and turn to face my mother. "I've been having the best sex of my life with someone who isn't my husband," I tell her. It's amazing how liberal you become with your mother when there is no filter to stop you from talking.

She lies there for a moment before she finally says, "That's nice, dear."

"It is. It really is. Pity he's a killer."

"A what, dear?"

"And he owns seggs clubs."

"Aka, sex clubs for those who don't say bad words," Simone yells.

"I know what she meant," my mother yells back to her, and Simone starts laughing again. "Do you like him?" she asks me.

"That's all you have to say?" I'm shocked that she isn't more concerned.

"Well, you were in an unhappy relationship, and I want you to be happy now. No matter what. But preferably with no more drugs, please."

"I don't do drugs." Then I wince when I realize she is talking about the brownie. "That was Simone..." I smile. "She's a bad influence on me. Plus, she's sleeping with Harvey, so you may get grandkids after all."

"Like hell," Simone yells.

To which my mother says, "In the next two years, please, while I can still help babysit and before I start traveling."

"I am *not* having kids," Simone replies.

"Sure, you aren't." I smile as another knock comes on the door.

"Gosh, does that door ever shut up?" Simone grumbles, getting off the couch to answer the incessant noise.

As she pulls it open, I look up.

Jake is standing there.

And his eyes are on mine.

CHAPTER 23
Who the fuck wants feelings?
JAKE

The smart thing to do is to stay away.

But for some stupid reason I keep getting drawn back to her. It's like someone has a noose around my neck and keeps pulling it tighter until I am with her, or near her, and I can finally breathe.

Who the fuck thinks like that about a woman.

Is this why fuckers get married, these stupid feelings they get.

Oriana likes to tell me to go away or to lose her number. But each and every time I see her, I know she is feeling whatever the fuck it is I am as well. Some sort of fucked up feelings.

"Who is that?" a lady lying next to Oriana asks. Her friend leaves the door open, and I step in. Oriana turns her head away from me and stares up at the ceiling.

174

"Aren't you meant to be... I don't know, making another happy?" she says.

"You mean...making her come?" I say smugly.

She waves a hand in the air. "Yeah, that." Everything goes silent before she says. "I told you to lose my number."

"It seems I keep getting drawn back to you, but when you said that, you never mentioned anything about showing up," I tell her. "I'm off to Italy soon. Would you care to accompany me?"

"Italy! Oh, how wonderful," the woman next to her exclaims. "You must go, Oriana. And bring me back some wine."

"Wine?" Oriana asks.

"Yes, wine. They have the *best* wine. Moscato, please, that's my pick."

Oriana rolls her eyes, and as I take in the kitchen, my gaze snags on a packet of brownies. I stride over and pick it up, then open the bag and take a smell. "You're high," I state, standing over her.

"Yep, and so is my mom." She points her thumb to the lady next to her.

"Your mother?" I ask surprised.

Fuck, meeting the mother.

"Yep. Bit early to meet the family, don't you think? But here you are." Oriana smiles, but it doesn't reach her eyes. I hide my smirk at the attitude she loves to give me. Her lids fall shut as she lies still and I glance at her mother, immediately seeing the resemblance.

"Nice to meet you. I'm Jake. I've taken Oriana here on a few dates," I say to her mother.

"Dates," Oriana says, giggling. "Dates where he seggses my brains out."

Lifting my hand to wipe the corner of my lips, I hide my smile at her outburst.

"Oriana!" her mother yells. Then she looks back at me with a kind smile. "Nice to meet you. This is Simone." She points to the woman on the couch. "Excuse Oriana, she's high and incapable of using the right words in such a state."

Oriana waves a hand in my direction. "He uses the right word. Why don't you tell my mother your favorite word?"

"Do you plan to lie on the floor the entirety of my visit?" I ask her.

"I didn't invite you, so yes! And you can leave any time." I look over my shoulder to see her friend asleep on the couch. Her mother is almost out too. And Oriana is giving me a death stare. "And tell your brother to leave me alone."

"I did. That's why I'm here. And to ask you about Italy, but you seem very distracted."

"Yes, you should leave." She waves a hand in the direction of the door before she sits up, crawls over to the counter, and pulls a pizza box down, opening it and eating a slice. Her mother starts to snore softly, and she giggles at her. "Why are you really here, Jake?" Her expression is questioning. "You told me to leave. And our dates are done, are they not?"

"Yes, they are," I answer.

"So, like I said, why are you here?" she asks again. She puts the pizza down and leans her head on the side of the counter.

"Are you okay?" I ask.

"I'm tired." Her eyes start to close, and she jolts as she starts to fall asleep sitting up. *Shit! How high is she?* I go back and shut the door, not one of them moving as I do. I pull a blanket from the couch, one that isn't covering her friend and place it over her mother before I bend down and reach for Oriana, picking up her light frame. Her arms go around my neck as I cradle her to me and I take her to her room. Clothes are everywhere, and her bed is a mess. Walking her over to it, I place her down then move her clothes out of the way.

"Jake," she mumbles sleepily.

"Hmm..." I lean down, brushing her red hair from her face.

"I hate that I like you." I smile at her words as she scoots over and opens her arms, her eyelids lifting just a little. "Cuddle me."

"I don't cuddle," I warn her.

"You do now. Now, cuddle me," she demands.

I kick off my shoes and climb into bed with her, then she flings a leg over me as she places her head on my chest.

"If I wasn't so drunk and high right now, we could totally do the nasty."

I brush her hair down with a laugh. "We can tomorrow," I tell her.

"Good. I like the nasty with you..." She pauses, nuzzling into me. "Do you like it with me?"

"Yes, every second of it." I don't know if she hears me because a soft snore leaves her mouth. Her grip loosens as she falls deeper into sleep.

I go to move, but she somehow knows and holds me tighter.

I don't sleep in the same room with anyone.

It's better that way.

Always has been.

So why do I not fight it when my eyes close?

Because I know I should.

Yet...

CHAPTER 24
Life flashes at weird times
ORIANA

I can't breathe.

My hands are scraping at his neck, and I can't breathe. Trying to scratch and pry his hands off me is doing nothing, and I can't reach his eyes. I feel myself getting lighter and lighter, the air leaving my body fully.

How is this possible?

How can he...

"Fuck, Oriana." The hands around my throat suddenly disappear.

I suck in a huge breath and manage to army crawl off my bed. *How did I get into this position?* I don't even know. I was sleeping, until I wasn't. I moved on him, and somehow, I got flipped onto my back, and the life was almost strangled out of me.

"Fuck." His hands go to his head and pull at his hair.

I crawl on the floor until I reach the corner, just barely holding myself together.

"Fuck, are you okay?" He makes to approach me, but I hold out my hand to stop him. "Oriana..."

"Y-you should leave. P-please leave..." I manage to gasp in some fresh air, but the pain in my neck makes it feel that much more painful.

"It's why I don't sleep with other people. I had..." He pauses. "Fuck, I told you I don't," he says it again, and this time he does leave, leaving me on the floor trying to gather air and stop the tingling sensation throughout my body. I blink a few times trying to get my bearings and as I'm about to get up, he suddenly walks back in with a bag of ice.

He cautiously walks over to me and holds it out. "My stepfather used to come in when I was sleeping and beat me." I'm so shocked by his admission that I sit there, stunned into a silent stupor. "When I got older, my first reaction was to reach out and grab what I could to protect myself. That is...until I took his life."

Jake sucks in a breath, still holding out the ice. "Take the ice, it will help your neck." I do as he says and place it on the front where it's currently burning. He scratches the back of his neck, looking nothing like the man I've come to know. "I didn't mean—"

"I get it." I don't get it completely, but I also do. He didn't mean to hurt me, yet he did.

Badly.

So badly that I think I'm going to have trouble sleeping next to anyone, ever again.

"You need to see someone," I tell him as I stand. "You can't do that again. You have to see someone."

"Yeah, that's what Cap says."

"He's right."

"It's never been an issue for me before. I never let another person sleep next to me," he tells me, and there's vulnerability in his voice. Something he never shares with me. He's always so...rude, crass, even vulgar sometimes. "I'll see someone," he finally says after a long pause, looking over his shoulder to the door. "No one is here..." He pauses unsure of his next move which is so unlike him. "They must have left. I should stay until someone can be here with you."

"No, please go," I beg. "They went to get break-fast." I heard them leave this morning; it's what woke me.

"Oriana."

"Jake, it's best you go," I say more forcefully. He nods, and this time he does leave, though I can tell by his expression it's the last thing he wants. I hear the front door close with a click before I get up and go straight for the shower. I sit down on the cold tiled floor and let the hot water pour over me.

Did that happen to him when he was very little?

And how could someone do that to a child?

I didn't know any of this about him, but then again, I don't really know much about him, as he keeps everything to himself.

A knock comes on the door, and my mother's voice filters through, letting me know they have breakfast when I'm done. Managing to stand and wash, I get out and dry off with my white, fluffy bath sheet. Looking in the mirror at my neck, which is red, I can already see that it's changing color. *Will it bruise?* I really hope not.

Sneaking back into my room, I grab a turtleneck and put it on before I join them. My mother smiles when she sees me, and there is no doubt Simone looks like death.

"We saw Jake leaving when we got back," my mother says. "He stayed the night?"

"He did," I answer and pull out a bagel from the bag on the counter. It's colorful and filled with the most delicious cream cheese imaginable—*birthday cake flavor.*

"So, you two are a thing?" she asks.

I look to Simone, who is also waiting to see what I say.

"We are *not* a thing. It was just—"

"Sex," Simone interrupts, to which I nod.

"I'm just saying that he seems guarded, from what I can tell. But his eyes, when he sees you, it's clear you aren't just a one-night stand to him."

I can't help but blush at my mother's words.

"He has demons, a lot of them, and I don't even know all of them," I reply, my chest tightening.

"Honey, we aren't meant to know every tidbit of everyone's lives. They choose to share with you out of love and respect..." She pauses, searching my eyes. "Did something happen to scare you away from him?"

My hand goes to my neck, but I don't want to tell her about that because that would mean I would defend him and tell her why he did it. And I have a feeling Jake doesn't share things like that openly.

"So, are you going to Italy with him?" Simone asks.

Wow! I forgot he'd asked me that question. And I can't believe I am even contemplating going. Because I am, but I'm not sure. I tell him to go away, but I also relish having him near me. What does that make me?

"I'll decide on Monday," I say, smiling. "This weekend, since Mom is here, let's go shopping."

"Oh, you know how I love to shop," Simone coos.

It's one of our favorite things to do together. She always gives the best fashion advice and is honest as all hell.

"I'm planning to pass back out and sleep the day away," Simone says. Just then, the door opens, and Harvey walks in. "Maybe I will go after all," she mumbles. Harvey smiles at Mom and me before he spots Simone. I'm not really sure about the status of what they are, and I don't plan on getting involved either. But I can tell by the way he is looking at Simone, he likes her, and she likes him too.

"Harvey, you'll keep Simone company, won't you, if your sister and I go shopping?" my mother asks as she kisses Harvey on the cheek.

"Of course I will," he agrees, without hesitation.

"Great. See you two later." I smile at both of them, and I notice Simone looks anywhere but at him while he stares openly at her.

As soon as we're outside, my mother starts to laugh. "They have it bad." See, she can see through anything and is always brutally honest. I used to hate it as a teenager, but somehow grew to appreciate it the older I got. When my friends would lie to me about clothes and small things to make me happy, or they'd tell me things they thought I wanted to hear, my mother never did. And I'm happy she's here.

"So, what happened with you and Kyler?" she asks as we reach the sidewalk.

"It was just too much, I think."

"Well, Kyler wasn't enough, so I think you may need to make a choice."

"Maybe."

"Nope. You pick either or neither. But those are your only options. And I'm pretty sure I know which way you are going."

"Oh, you do?" I ask, raising a brow.

"Of course. I'm your mother. I know you best."

"And who, or which way, will I choose?" I ask as we walk along the street before we stop at a cute little boutique.

"I'll never tell, but I heard it's chilly this time of year in Italy. Better find you a scarf," she teases, and I laugh.

Sometimes a girl simply needs her mother.

WHEN MY MOTHER LEAVES, I almost want to tell her to stay. It's good to have that person who constantly has your back, no strings, just your own personal rock star. I had a real rock star, but that didn't turn out great for me.

I don't hear from Jake at all that week. When he does finally decide to contact me, it's Friday, and he's waiting for me at my house. I stop when I see him, my keys clutched in my hand.

"Oriana." He says my name like he would if he was hovering over the top of me—full of seduction. "I'm leaving for Italy in an hour. I was hoping you would come." His offer, and the timing, shocks me.

"You didn't say when, just soon."

"Maybe it's time you see what I do. And then, when you return, if you choose not to see me again, I'll do my best to respect your wishes." I bite my bottom lip as I contemplate his words. "Do you have plans?" he asks.

"No."

"And Monday is a public holiday, so you don't have to work." I nod in confirmation.

"Why now? I've asked you before to leave me alon—"

He cuts me off. "You've never meant it before, Oriana. I've seen all sides of you, and you've never meant it, yet."

"So next time, if I don't like what I see, you'll what, leave me be?"

"If that's what you chose," he states, but his voice doesn't sound convincing. Should it, though?

"I'll pack a bag," I tell him, then turn to go inside. He doesn't follow me in, but I leave the door unlocked for him anyway. I throw some clothes in my small suitcase and grab what I need from the bathroom before I head back outside. Jake's checking his phone when I walk up to him and say, "Ready." He glances at me and then eyes my bag.

"That's the fastest I have *ever* seen a woman pack." He sounds impressed as he holds out his hand for my overnight bag. I let him take it, and he places it in the trunk before he opens the door for me. My eyes follow him as he walks around to his side of the car and slides in.

"What airline are we flying?" I ask. I grab my passport out of my bag to double-check it's there.

"We fly private. You'll understand on the way back why," he says as he starts the car.

Kyler used to fly private or first class. I never really got to go on many of his trips. It was always him and his staff while I ran everything from home. It's nice to be asked to go somewhere instead of honestly, being left behind without a thought.

We hardly speak on the drive. I can feel his energy though, and although he's silent and I know he's unsure of what to say to me and I feel the exact same way. When we finally arrive at the airport, it's an easy process being led to the private plane. We get on, and he sits opposite me.

"Do you want to talk about it?" he asks.

The flight attendant offers us each a glass of champagne. He declines, and I take it happily.

"Talk?" I ask before drinking the entire glass of

bubbly liquid. As soon as it's gone, I look over my shoulder and ask for another. When I turn back around, he's in my face, and he pulls down the neckline of my shirt. He winces when he sees the marks, then his eyes find mine, and I see the sorrow in them when he closes them for a few seconds with a deep, centering breath.

"Does it hurt?" The gentleness and concern in his voice surprises me.

"No," I tell him. "It doesn't hurt."

He lets go of my shirt, and it falls back into place as he sits back down. I take the second glass of champagne being offered to me and drink it down just as quickly as the first.

"Have you become an alcoholic since I saw you last?" he asks, smiling.

"Flying makes me nervous."

"You should have told me. I could have gotten you something."

I hold up the glass and say, "This works just fine."

"If you say so." He smiles.

We take off, and one of my hands grips the armrest while the other holds the champagne glass tight enough that it could break at any moment. Jake studies me silently as we rise into the air. Then as soon as the light comes on, letting us know we can move about, I'm turning back to search for the flight attendant and asking for another glass before a thought occurs to me and I blurt out the words before I can even think, "You aren't like a human trafficker, are you? You don't plan to sell me when we get off this plane, right?"

"I don't plan to sell you. You're too expensive to get rid of."

"I'm actually not." I smile as I receive another glass.

"Irreplaceable," I hear him mutter under his breath. The champagne has finally kicked in, and I'm feeling a little better as I unbuckle myself. "There's a bed in the back if you're tired."

"Is that where you sleep with other people?" I ask.

"No, I told you..." *Oh yes, he doesn't sleep with anyone, he only has sex with them.* "I've been seeing someone." When those words leave his mouth, my heart stops, and my body locks tight as I reach the door that leads to the bedroom.

Seeing someone.

Is that what we do?

See other people?

I guess we never said we were exclusive, so that's only fair, but I had hoped...

Then again, all we had was sex.

Great sex.

There was little else other than that when I really think about it.

Turning back around, I see him watching me for a reaction.

"You aren't going to say anything?" he asks.

"Do you need a congratulations?" I ask, angry and confused. "I haven't been seeing anyone else. I didn't know we did that."

"I haven't been fucking anyone else, Oriana. I meant seeing a therapist... To help me."

Oh. Oh, sugar, now I feel bad. But happy he is doing that. Is it for me? Or him? I hope it's for him.

"Is it helping?"

"I've only had two sessions, but yes, I think it may be." His fingers strum on the seat.

"Good," I whisper.

Then I head for the bedroom and pass out on the bed.

CHAPTER 25

Get your tits out

JAKE

O riana doesn't answer when I knock on the door. She's been in there for the duration of the flight, and I haven't seen her. I thought I would give her some space, not realizing she was a nervous flyer.

I probably should have asked her the question.

But this is all new to me.

Not once in my life have I had a romantic relationship with someone.

I fuck.

And I like to fuck.

I'm even good at fucking.

But this—*she*—is all new to me.

I'm not sure exactly where the shift came from or when I started wanting her for more than sex. But it's there, heavy as all fuck, like a massive burden and it is

191

all her. How would I take it if she chose not to see me again? I would try to respect her decision, but fuck, that would be hard.

Knocking again, I wait for Oriana to answer before pushing the door open. I find her sprawled out over the bed—her hair a wild mess having fallen out from her bun—and sound asleep. Stepping closer, I touch her leg. "Oriana." She doesn't move. I sit on the bed next to her and gently shake her shoulder. "Oriana..."

She stirs, and when she does, her top shifts, and her breasts fall out.

Fuck.

"Oriana," I say again, louder now. She opens her eyes and stretches. "Your tits are out." She looks down and automatically pulls up her shirt. Rising to sit, she reaches to the other side of the bed and picks up her bra, and slides it on underneath her shirt, doing that girly thing they do when putting on or pulling off a bra using the shirt for modesty.

"I can't sleep with my bra on. They dig in," she says quietly, getting up. "Are we there?"

"We are," I answer and sit for a moment as she sweeps out of the room. I hear Maria's voice, so I stand and go out to greet her. Both ladies turn to me and walk up the aisle.

"I didn't realize you were bringing company on this trip," Maria comments.

"Yes. Maria, meet Oriana." I wave my hand at Maria. "Maria is my cousin," I tell Oriana, then add, "And my assistant."

"Oh, nice to meet you." Oriana offers her hand, but Maria ignores it. "Well, okay then."

"You didn't say you were bringing anyone. Does she know why we're here?" Maria asks.

"Say fucking hello, Maria." I nod to Oriana.

Maria looks to Oriana and gives her the wort half-assed "Hello," then her focus is back on me. "Happy now? One of the parties has already started. Is she accompanying you? And if so, she can't wear *that*." She nods at what Oriana is wearing.

"Did you bring a dress?" I ask Maria.

"I did."

"Good, give it to her."

"That's *my* dress," she argues.

"Now it's Oriana's," I bite back to her. She is the only woman I fight this much with. I think she secretly likes it. But Maria is good, and family. It's why I didn't fire her ass long ago.

"I don't have to wear your dress," Oriana says to Maria, then she turns to me. "Don't make Maria give me her dress. It's hers."

"Technically, it's mine. I paid for it. Maria has plenty of dresses, all bought with my money."

"I do. Every time he pisses me off, I go and buy

something outrageous because he doesn't know how to apologize." She shrugs, smiling. "It's fine. You need a dress, and I have another." She walks off the plane without another word.

"Is it fancy?" Oriana asks, playing with her hair. "Do I need makeup?"

"You never have," I answer her as Maria comes back, holding a light blue, floor-length dress.

"Wow, that's beautiful," Oriana gushes as she takes it from Maria.

"It is, isn't it?" Maria smiles. "Will look better on you, I'm sure."

"We'll wait in the car outside. When you're dressed, meet us there," I tell Oriana.

"When did you change?" she asks, nodding to my suit.

"While you slept," I reply before I head off the plane. Maria follows and leans against my car as we wait.

"You brought a date? Really?" She laughs. "She seems too nice for this world."

"She is."

"Are you sure she can handle it?" Maria asks.

"It's the reason I brought her. I figured she'd never want to see me again after she found out whose house I took her to, but here she is."

"And your brother?"

"Yes, about him..."

"I checked. It seems he's left." I nod, thankful Maria is on top of everything. It's another reason I don't fire her ass.

Oriana catches my attention as she steps off the plane. The gown is long and ties up around her neck. She has put her hair up into a bun on top of her head and is wearing a light shade of lipstick.

"It's absolutely your dress. It looks one hundred times better on you than me," Maria tells her, then winks before she gets into the passenger side of the car. I hold the door open to the back seat as Oriana steps past me and glides in. The dress is backless. God have mercy, her back is sexy.

When she's seated, she looks up at me and asks, "Am I dressed okay?"

I nod and close her door before I walk around and slide in next to her.

"A few things..." I start. She turns her body to face me paying full attention to my words. "Don't interact with any of the men. Stay by my side or Maria's." I nod to Maria in the front, who is currently sliding on a dress without a care in the world.

"Why?" she asks.

I ignore Oriana's question and continue, "Second, do not, and I repeat... *Do not* tell anyone your name or where you are from."

"Okay, this is sounding weird now." She balls her hands in her lap and starts to rub them together nervously.

"If you see something seedy, it more than likely is. Women are objects in this place. Remember that. And don't speak to them either."

She sits back and stares out the window.

She's either going to run for the hills or...

CHAPTER 26

Respect, really? How about you just bend me over?

ORIANA

What was I thinking? I should have asked more questions when Jake invited me to go with him. It would have been the smart thing to do. But I stupidly said yes without getting more information. It's been a while since I traveled and I was excited.

I shouldn't have been.

Because I don't know what I have gotten myself into.

The car comes to a stop out front of a large house with a garden that the car has to drive around before a man opens the door. I get out, and Jake comes around and stands next to me, offering me his arm. I slide my hand into the crook of his elbow as we walk up the large staircase leading into the house. Two armed guards stand on the outside and nod to Jake as he enters.

What is going on here?

I don't think I've been to a party where guards stand so visibly holding guns.

Gripping Jake's arm a little tighter, we head inside, with me sandwiched between him and Maria. I audibly gasp when we enter. The lingering smell of cigar smoke and whiskey is overpowering. There are quite a few women who are all dressed the same—in black dresses —and their eyes are downcast as the men walk around freely eyeing them. A few turn to look at us. Some hold our eyes, while others simply look away and continue whatever it is they're doing.

"Jake," someone calls in a thick Italian accent.

I find the man instantly and see him already watching me. He speaks in Italian, which I have no idea what he's saying, but Jake looks at me and smiles.

"The lady speaks English, so let's speak that out of respect for her." I smile at both of them, and the man offers his hand. I place my hand in his, and he leans down and kisses it.

"Jake only ever brings the darling Maria with him." His eyes flick to Maria before they come back to me. "It's nice to see he is human, after all."

"Leonardo," Jake warns, and Leonardo drops my hand and gives his attention to Jake.

"How many are we after tonight?" Leonardo asks.

"Two."

"Good, good." Leonardo nods his head and turns away. "This way." He motions for us to follow him, and Maria stays close by the whole time. I glance back at her when, all of a sudden, Jake stops and grips my arm tight.

"Why are you here?" Jake snarls.

And when I face forward again, I see his brother standing there. A drink in hand and a smirk on his face.

Leonardo is the first to speak, "This is your brother?" he asks, confused while Grayson stands there, smiling.

"If you can give us a minute?" Jake asks Leonardo, who glances between the two and then walks out of the room, leaving the four of us together. Grayson's eyes flick to me, and I can see the mischief in them before he looks back to Jake.

"You have a thing for redheads now," Grayson comments. "You even brought her with you."

"What are you doing here? You weren't invited," Jake bites back, ignoring Grayson's words.

"Oh, come on, brother, you know you want me here." He goes to touch Jake's shoulder, but Jake pulls back, not allowing him to touch him. "Still have an issue with being touched, I see." His eyes flick to me, and I feel guilty automatically, but Jake says nothing, just glances back at Maria.

"Have him escorted out," Jake orders.

"You always had a thing for being in charge. I'm staying, brother. Or...I will come back and visit, and your friends will not be happy." Jake grinds his molars. "Now, show me how this works." Grayson taps Jake's shoulder, making Jake pull away, then he walks past us and out the door.

Jake's eyes find mine, and when I search them, I see hate. It's directed at me, though there is definitely an undercurrent of distrust toward his brother. Maria leaves the room, and Jake and I are left by ourselves.

"Jake."

He turns to face me but says nothing.

The anger is simmering in his dark eyes, and so I ask, "Do you want to leave? We can go to a hotel," I offer, trying to calm him.

"You didn't even want me around you a few days ago!" He growls, and my hand drops from his arm at his anger that's now firmly directed at me. "Don't act like you care now." I'm so taken aback by his words that I have to remember he's upset, and it isn't just directed at me.

I hope.

I stand there as he silently clenches his jaw, waiting for me to speak.

But what can I say?

Instead, I do what I want to do. I reach up and grip

his face. He doesn't pull away from me, he merely stands there still like a statue.

Stepping closer to him, I lean in and kiss his cheek, moving slowly with small kisses until I reach his mouth. When my lips press against the corner of his lips, I feel him jolt, and I stop instantly. I pull back, and my hands slide down from his face to his chest, going lower and lower until I reach the belt on his trousers. Then I slip my hand a little lower and cup his dick.

"Hotel?" I ask him again.

"You are dangerous," he whispers, leaning in and kissing the side of my neck. I squeeze my hand around his erection, and he groans. "I have to work. But after, if you still want to be fucked, I'll fuck you." I nod and drop my hands to my sides as Maria opens the door.

"They're waiting," she announces. Guilt swarms Maria's face, but she hides it just as fast as I see it.

Jake offers me his hand and leads me out of the room, stopping at a guy with two girls by his side. Jake reaches for the first girl's chin and lifts it so he can see her face. Her expression is blank, and she looks anywhere but at him.

"This one is good... compliant. She'll do what you say," the man standing with the girls says. "Tell him," he orders the girl.

"Yes, Master." Her voice is lifeless, and her whole demeanor screams soullessness.

Jake looks at the man. "Give me five minutes with both."

The man walks away, leaving the women with us.

What is going on here?

And why did they call him Master?

"Is this a life you would like to stay in, or would you like one where you are in control of your body and can earn your freedom?" The women have a silent conversation with their eyes before they turn to Jake.

"Is this a trick question?" the one he touched asks.

"No. I want to know if you will agree to sell your body, at your own choice, and work in a club of mine. The contract is for one year, and you can choose to stay or leave when your time is up. But for the price I pay for you, you have to work it off. Do you understand?"

I can see the confusion written all over their faces when their eyebrows scrunch together, and I'm pretty sure it mirrors mine. They turn around and search for the man who was standing with them before they look back at Jake.

"If this is real, then yes," she answers for both of them.

Maria leans in and whispers something in Jake's ear before she glances at me and then tells the ladies to follow him. I'm not really one hundred percent sure what is happening right now, and I don't think it's the right time to ask any questions.

Jake's hand slips into mine, and then we make our way through the room again. A few men greet him, and I can tell he's quite popular and even respected.

He keeps me by his side the whole night. Talking to two more women, he basically asks them the same question he asked the first two. He's a mystery, and I realize in small amounts he is letting me in but not giving me the full story.

Attending an event with Jake is different from attending one with Kyler. Jake asked me questions and included me in conversations when he was talking to people—never giving too much detail about who I am or where I'm from. With Kyler, I was arm candy and was expected to remain silent.

When the night starts to slow, and he's made his rounds and talked to almost everyone in the room, I excuse myself to find the bathroom. I end up in the kitchen, where there is a group of women huddled together, talking. I hear the end of the conversation and freeze where I am standing.

"Do you think she's one of his working girls?" one asks.

Another one shakes her head before she answers, "I highly doubt it. Unless she runs the place and fucks him on the side."

I gasp, knowing they are talking about me.

The one who asked the question turns around and spots me, and I back into the hall, letting the door shut behind me. I turn to continue my search for the bathroom, but I accidentally bump into someone. A hand grips my bare shoulder, stopping me from moving away. The man reeks of alcohol, and his smile sends shivers all over my body.

"I've seen you before," he slurs.

I try to hold my breath as he speaks because he stinks. The man grips my shoulder even tighter and pushes me back. I go to move away, but for someone so intoxicated, he is fast and slams my back against the wall.

I have felt intimidated before in my life, but never quite like this. In this situation right now, I feel more scared than I was that night in that alleyway, though I have hardly any recollection of that incident. My body freezes and my mind starts to go blank as he whispers close to my ear, "I wonder how much it would cost to have you for the night?"

My hands lift, and I try to shove him away, but he simply laughs at my efforts and pushes me back against the wall once more, but harder this time.

"With that type of attitude, I think I should get you for free." His hand flexes at my neck before he adds, "Don't you?"

I can't even fathom the words to speak to him right now. My mind is blank, and I feel a panic attack is coming on. He leans in, his breath on my neck, and that's when I feel his lips touch my skin.

"Get off of me." It was meant to be a scream, but it comes out as a breathy gasp.

He chuckles and leans his full body, so it presses on me. A tear leaves my eye, and I hear the laughter of the women from the room right next to me.

Why is no one coming out?

Why is no one doing anything?

I watch in disbelief from where I am pinned against the wall as a man walks by, glances in my direction, and keeps on going. Then a server comes out of the kitchen and looks in our direction. I ask him for help, but he quickly turns away and hurries down the hall.

The only thing left I can think of to do is to scream for Jake. But for some strange reason, words refuse to leave my mouth, no matter how hard I try. I squeeze my eyes shut, and suddenly, the man is no longer there.

Before I can open my eyes, I feel relief and then see Jake standing before me, holding the other man by his neck. Jake's dark eyes search mine before they drop to my body, and I watch as they turn almost black. "Are you okay?" he asks me.

I go to answer, but the drunk man starts laughing.

Jake turns his attention to him.

"Is this a joke? You parade her around for what? I'll pay. You know I'm good for it," the man says.

Jake ignores him and looks back at me, asking, "Did. He. Hurt. You?"

"She's a whore. She deserves to be hurt," the man declares, and Jake's eyes slice to him again.

"I'd watch what you say, Mercedes," Jake warns.

The man laughs again. "Are you catching feelings for the whore? I heard you kicked out your brother, yet you let a whore stay." He goes to pull away and tries to reach for me again.

Everything happens so fast, and it takes me a moment to process it all. From my spot against the wall, I see Jake pull out a knife and drag it across the man's throat, then Jake steps away as the man falls to the floor in a heap, trying to stop the blood from pouring out of his wound.

Jake offers me his hand, but I don't know if I can take it. I'm frozen in shock as I watch the man struggle on the ground. Another server comes by but doesn't slow down or say anything.

Jake gives up, waiting for me to take his hand and reaches for me, then tugs me away. I move on autopilot as he guides me with his strong grip, my adrenaline coursing through every vein before I realize we're in the safety of his car.

CHAPTER 27

Don't touch what's mine

JAKE

Did I think tonight would go as I hoped? Of course I did. But it didn't go as I had hoped—it went the complete fucking opposite.

Mercedes should've known to keep his hands to himself, but the old grump always touches what he shouldn't. He thinks having a shitload of money and power allows him to do whatever the fuck he pleases. How wrong he was. To say I hadn't thought of slitting that man's throat when I first met him would be a complete and utter lie. The number of women I have purchased from him, well, let's just say he's fucking disgusting. That man needed to learn some respect. But he was never going to learn it on his own, so I showed him exactly what type he deserves.

Oriana sits frozen next to me. I don't know what

to say to her, so I let her be and give her the space she needs on the car ride to the hotel. Her hands are tucked on her lap, and I can see her visibly shaking.

I reach for her, but she pulls away.

She's too good for me.

I knew that from the moment I saw her, but I couldn't stay away, no matter how hard I tried. And believe me, I did fucking try.

But when I saw her at that event, dressed in *that dress* and up on the stage, I just knew I couldn't say no. I knew I had to bid on her, and I knew I would win. They say I am the king of bidding, not because I can outbid anyone, but because I always fucking win. Her being married at the time did *not* stop me one tiny bit.

We reach the hotel, and Maria is already there. She opens Oriana's door, and she is quick to escape the car. Maria raises her brow, and all I say is "Mercedes." She gives me her best eye roll before she follows Oriana inside.

I'm not sure if I should give her more breathing room or not, but I find her standing in the lobby, twirling her hair a sure sign of her wariness of what's going to happen next.

Unsure of what to do, I walk over and place my hand on the small of her back. She doesn't flinch, which I'm thankful for. Her eyes lock on mine, and I can see the confusion and pain in those rainforest greens staring back at me.

"I would never let anyone hurt you. I hope you know that," I tell her sincerely. She stares silently at me, and I pull her hand from her hair and hold it loosely in mine. "Are you scared of me?"

Thick, long lashes fan her cheeks when she closes her eyes and takes a deep inhale. On the exhale, her lids raise, and those beautiful eyes once again find mine.

"I'm not scared of you, Jake. I'm more…" She's trying to search for the right word. "Shocked. Shocked that you could so easily do *that*." She shakes her head, and I reach for her hip, pulling her to me. She comes easily, and I wrap my arms around her.

"I'd do it again." No lies are hidden in my response, and I know she can see that she knows.

"This is all a lot."

And I agree. It would be very much for someone who has lived in a perfect little bubble her whole life and never had to do anything other than survive in that bubble. She doesn't understand the workings of the underground, and I'm so thankful that she doesn't. Oriana may be strong, of that, I have no doubt—I witnessed her pull herself back together after a night that would break most people—but I knew I had to show her the dark side because I want her. I want her more than my next fucking breath, and I absolutely hate that fact, but I also relish it.

"Everything that happened back there is a part of who I am. I am not, nor will I ever be, anything like your rock star husband." She goes to speak, but I shake my head and continue, "You had the perfect life with him, but you weren't happy. You do realize this, don't you? I've seen more life from you since I've been with you than I did prior to knowing you."

"You didn't know me before?"

I smile at her question because even if she never saw me, I always saw her. From the moment she walked down that aisle and married Kyler, I thought, *How does a son of a bitch like that get her?* He never deserved her. He used her and worked her to the bone. And he had other women on the side—of which I'm sure she has no idea about. Every time I saw him with a woman who wasn't Oriana, I would wonder, *what is that pretty little redhead doing right now?*

"You were beautiful in your wedding dress," is the only response I can give her right now.

"I forgot Kyler said you were at our wedding. How and why were you there?"

"Do you want to sightsee tomorrow?" I ask, changing the subject completely.

Her mood has visibly shifted, and the tightness she was holding onto has relaxed just a little.

She replies with a simple "sure" and I take her hand and guide her to our suite. I ordered a room with two bedrooms, but I really hope—*really fucking hope*—that she'll share the same bed with me, even if it's only for a few hours.

Because the last thing I want to do is wake up with my hands around her neck again.

CHAPTER 28

Sit on it and call me Daddy

ORIANA

W hen we get to the room, our bags are already there. Jake goes to a set of double doors and pulls them open. When I follow, I realize it's a connecting room.

"You can have your space," he says.

I'm not really sure what to say, so I simply nod before I pass him and step into the room. He follows not long after, carrying my bag and placing it on the bed, and then he leaves me alone. I don't bother shutting the doors as I unzip my bag and pull out my pajamas and toothbrush. I'm guessing the reason he got connecting rooms is because the last time he fell asleep in my vicinity, he woke up with his hands around my neck, choking the life right out of me.

He explained a little of it, but there is way more to

the story. I'm sure I don't even know the half of it, but the part I do know is troubling.

I strip out of my dress, go into the bathroom, and start the shower. Stepping under the spray, I let the hot water rain over me, then I scrub my shoulders and neck where that man touched me, thinking I could get the feel of him out of my mind. It partly works until I hear a knock at the door, and my body freezes. But as soon as Jake's voice carries through into the bathroom, every muscle relaxes. I should be terrified after what I had just witnessed, but that isn't my natural reaction to him.

"I've ordered room service. You need to eat."

Come to think of it, I've hardly eaten all day. Though my stomach starts grumbling for food, I finish up in the shower, washing my face, and then quickly changing into my pajamas.

When I walk out of my room, Jake's seated at a table covered with plates of food. He doesn't notice me at first, as he's on his phone typing away, but then all of a sudden, his dark eyes meet mine. He's not a man who will simply offer you a smile. No, instead, he stares at you as if he can see straight into your soul.

"Eat," he commands and places his phone down. I sit across from him and notice the phone lighting up with several messages all at once. He doesn't even touch it, just watches me, waiting for me to eat. I open the first cloche, and the smell of pasta instantly hits me. My stomach gives a loud grumble, and Jake smirks before he opens another cloche that contains a Margherita pizza. He serves me a drink, and I waste no time as I start eating. He digs into his own dish, and we both groan at the taste of the best pasta in the world.

"Do you want to run?" I didn't quite expect that question. And to be honest, a part of me did want to run, and I'm really unsure why the other part wants to stay.

"Not yet," I reply, as it's the only response I can think to give.

"I'd never let another man touch you without your consent. You get that, right?"

I do. I really do get it, and I feel the words he's speaking are the truth.

"Tell me why we were there. I want to hear you say it. I have my own assumptions, and I want you to correct them if I'm wrong."

"If you eat, I'll tell you."

I place a forkful of pasta into my mouth all the while watching him with eager eyes waiting for him to speak. .

He wastes no time with his response. "I'm in the business of sex. You've gathered that much, as I never hide the fact from you of what I do. But how these women come to work for me... it's not something that

I openly share with everyone because, to state the fact, it's no one else's fucking business but mine and theirs."

He pauses, and I wait to hear what he says next.

"There is a very large underground market here where high-profile people buy and sell women. Most of these women are abducted, and then they are broken down into small pieces of themselves that only they can fix.

"And these women will wake up having been used and abused. Some are beyond help, but for those who aren't, I buy them. Which really makes me no better than the devils who took them in the first place. The difference is this devil gives them an opportunity for a better life, but it comes with a price tag, make no mistake. I give them a choice to sell their bodies. They pick who they sleep with if that's something they are comfortable doing. If not, they go behind the bar, the front of the house, or whatever I have available, but they are still in this game of sex. Because I pay millions of dollars for these women, and I expect to get that money back.

"I am no hero, Oriana. I have reasons why I do this. Some of them are selfish, and some of them are not. And if you ask me to stop doing this tomorrow, I wouldn't. I've been doing this for as long as I've owned my sex club. It's costly to be me. So you see, the evil part of me still keeps these women bound by chains, even though the life I have given them is a hundred times better than the life they were living. At least with me, they will not be abused, no man will ever disrespect them in my presence, they get their own place, they choose their own hours, and once their debt is paid off, they can choose to stay or leave."

He leans in close, my heart beating wildly at all this new information he is sharing. "Oriana, most of them choose to stay. Not out of any other reason than they actually enjoy it. They like having their control back, and that is exactly what I'm giving them... control of their own lives. Some might say it's fucked-up control, but the women know they can leave at any given time once their debt is paid.

"I never claimed to be an angel, Oriana. I am anything but. And in a lot of people's stories, I am the villain. Even in your story, I may very well be that when our time comes to an end. But I've given you—correction—I've *shown* you more of myself than I have ever let another human being see. Not even Maria or Captain, who are the closest people to me, know half the shit I have gone through. They simply think I never let a woman spend the night because I don't want attachments. But what they don't know is I do it out of simple self-defense. I could kill you quite easily before I even open my eyes. And I hope to never ever do that."

I cover my mouth with my hand to hold back the sob that wants to escape and simply sit there, staring at him. I can tell he's waiting for me to say something, but I just can't think of a single response to what he's shared.

He took me to this place, knowing that women are seen as nothing but objects. Granted, he did warn me not to leave his side, and I didn't listen. I should've asked more questions. I should have dug deeper. I'm a little blind when it comes to Jake, but not in the same way I was with my husband. Jake shares things with me and tells me things, whereas Kyler hardly ever talked to me unless it had to do with his career. It was always me trying to pry information from him.

I know it's not fair to compare the two—they are completely different—but Kyler was all I knew until Jake, so it's hard not to. And at first with Jake, I thought it may have been just about sex, but I've come to realize it's so much more than that. My feelings for him have grown over time, and I think if I don't leave soon, those feelings will turn into something more. And I really don't want to be a broken mess ever again.

"You can speak," he says.

I suck air between my teeth, unsure of what to say. "I think I just need to sleep," I tell him.

"You have nothing you want to say?" he asks.

I look down at my food, then answer, with a firm,

"No." I stand and push my seat back. I'm trying my best not to look at him as I walk in the direction of my room, but when he says my name, I can't help but meet his eyes.

"Can I join you?" he asks quietly.

I should tell him no. I mean, he did just tell me that he buys women for the sex trade. But for some reason, I give a simple, soft "yes" and continue on to my room. I hear his chair scrape across the floor as he gets up and follows me. I climb into bed, and he lifts the sheets and climbs in straight after me. Jake's hand finds my hip, and he turns me, so I'm no longer on my side but on my back. He gets up real close to my ear and whispers, "If you want me to stop, say so now."

I say nothing. His touch is something I welcome, and he knows it.

"I'll take that as an invitation." His hand slides under the waistband of my pants. When I lift my gaze to his face, I find him watching me.

"It's so wrong," I whisper.

"But it feels so right," he says, slipping his hand even farther down. I lift my hips as he pushes the pants from me and then gets up, kicking the blanket away and hovering over me.

"What are we?" I ask him. "What is this?"

He smirks, dropping down and pushing my shirt up my stomach.

"It's just sex, right?" I whisper, but he says nothing as he starts to kiss my stomach.

I hate that I get so lost in him.

How can someone make you forget about all the wrongs and only see them?

He's all I see when he touches me—just him.

One hand slides up under my shirt and between my breasts until he reaches my throat. He squeezes either side of my neck lightly, and I lift my hips as his tongue touches me down there.

"Just sex?" I hear him mutter, but his mouth and tongue don't stop moving. "With only, ever you," he whispers, but I can no longer form words as he holds me in place with his hand on my neck, slightly applying pressure, and the fingers of the other slide into me with a beautiful rhythm I didn't know he could produce. Every time he touches me, it feels like something brand new.

Sex with Jake is one of my favorite things.

I never knew a woman could have so many spots that turn her on.

Those words show how sheltered I was.

How dull my sex life was.

I wouldn't say my sex life before was bad, just not spicy. We had sex, and that was the extent of it.

With Jake, I'm down for trying everything.

The hand around my throat right now proves it.

Because though he applies pressure, he does it tenderly. *I wonder if he is showing me that he won't hurt me.* Especially, considering how we woke up last time we were in a bed together.

"Holy..."

"Shit," he finishes, his tongue stroking me like I'm his favorite meal.

He slides his fingers in and out as I come around them, not stopping until I feel completely spent. He removes his fingers and crawls up my body, letting go of my throat and gazing down at me.

"Ride me," he demands and flips me over, so I'm straddling him. He drops his hands and puts them behind his head as he watches me.

"What are you doing?" I ask.

"You have it."

"Have what?" I'm confused.

"Full control. Show me what you want."

I feel him under me, not in me, but near me. I slide lower until I see his penis between my legs, and then I reach down and touch it. He smirks, and I start to grind on it, not inserting his length but letting it rub my clit. I almost forget that I'm using him until he hisses, and I open my eyes to see he hasn't moved, but his bare stomach is now taut with restraint. I can tell he wants to move his hands to touch me.

"What would you give me if I slipped you inside

me right now?" I ask, slowing down my hips. Teasing him at my entrance. He bites his bottom lip, and I roll my hips again, this time extra slow.

"Whatever it is that you want," he grits out.

"A kiss," I whisper.

"Anything but that," he replies.

I ignore him and continue to slide my hips back and forth. He goes to move his hands, and I stop.

"Don't touch me. I didn't give you permission," I say, smirking.

He groans but does as I say. I pull my shirt over my head, freeing my breasts, and my hand on his penis holds him there as I continue to my languid grind. His piercing rubs me perfectly as I reach the tip but don't yet sink down on him. I cup my breast and squeeze my nipple, pulling it.

"It feels so good," I whisper. "So, *so* good." My head lolls back, and all I want to do is let him fill me, but I don't want him to hold all the power.

He has to give a little to get a little.

And riding his cock like this still feels like heaven.

"Fuck it!" He growls. "This is going to cost you."

Before I can even ask what he's talking about, he leans up, and his mouth slams onto mine. My body freezes as our lips mold together, then his tongue slithers into my mouth, and he kisses me. I can taste myself, but what I can taste more is him.

All him.

And holy heck, Jake can kiss.

His tongue dances with mine as he pulls back, bites my lip, and does it all over again. I somehow manage to maintain consciousness instead of letting that kiss knock me out and reach down and glide him into me. His lips pause on mine as I do, and when I sink down on him fully, he seems to remember where we are and what we're doing, then he kisses me again.

I've been kissed before.

Touched before.

Possibly even loved before.

Yet nothing, *nothing* compares to Jake.

And the thought scares the absolute shit out of me.

CHAPTER 29

Money makes my words spin, so does she

JAKE

Her back is to me while she lies sleeping beside me. I reach for her and pull her into my chest.

With her warm body pressed against me, the last thing I want to do is move. But I know I have to. I can't risk falling asleep next to her again, not after last time.

She is the only person in this world where it physically pains me to hurt her. It's an ache that sits deep in my chest.

It reminds me of my mother—I hated her but loved her regardless.

She was like the women I buy.

It's why I do what I do.

My father, a rich sociopath, left her after he found out she was pregnant with me, and she was no longer useful to him. She did what she could to survive, even if that meant letting the devil himself sleep in a place a child should feel safe—a home.

Letting Oriana think she is unsafe near me is not an option. The fact she can trust me enough to fall asleep next to me tells me so. I lift the blanket and pull it up over her as I get out of the bed. She makes a soft sound but doesn't wake as I turn off the light and shut the door.

I go to my phone and find several missed calls from Maria. Calling her back, she immediately swears at me when she answers, followed by, "Your brother is down here at the hotel bar. Please come," then hangs up. I dress and reach for my knife, tucking it into my pants before I head down there.

There is no love lost between my brother and me. I could easily slice that man's throat, brother or not, and not lose one minute of sleep.

I don't always choose violence. There are enough people who can do that for me. But if it comes down to it, I have no issue dealing with it myself.

Entering the bar area, Maria's holding a glass as she sits next to Grayson. Grayson leans in and says something to her, she pushes him away, and he laughs. I stalk over to them, and they both turn to face me when I'm only a few feet away.

"You were escorted out. Clearly, you missed the exit sign," I say to Grayson.

He holds up his drink. "I was escorted out of your little gathering, but this is a public bar that you *do not own*, brother."

"We are hardly brothers. Blood means fuck all," I tell him.

"This I know."

I cross my arms over my chest. "Do you, though? Because I still see you following me around like a bad smell."

My brother chooses to ignore me and taps his fingers on the counter, indicating for another drink. He nods to Maria before he waves his hand at me. "And whatever he drinks," he tells the bartender. The bartender looks at me, and I shake my head.

"The hunters won't be impressed if I come back empty-handed. They may very well tell me to go straight back to your town. Do you think the men who protect you can really defend you against them?" he asks.

I don't know the hunters, but their stories are hard to believe.

But I have no doubt what they say is true.

They are evil.

And they also like to collect.

"What do they want?" I ask.

He smirks. "They want your women."

"For what?"

He takes a sip of his drink before answering, "For whatever it is they please. I don't ask dumb questions."

"Why would you not ask questions?" I say to him.

"I don't get paid enough to ask questions, that's why."

"So it's money. That's the real reason you're here."

"Money is the ruler of this world, is it not?" he argues.

"Is it really the hunters who want the women, or do you want them for your clubs?" I question.

He offers me a smile. "You got me there. The hunters would have nothing to do with such things." I grind my teeth. "Though, I want to collect a few women like you do." He nods to Maria. "You both have the resources, so give me a woman."

"It doesn't work like that," I argue. "I don't collect women. I buy them—"

"It does. I'll pay. You know I'm good for it. Call it what you want."

Maria scoffs, and Grayson turns to her as she raises a brow. "Don't look at me, you dickhead." She growls while I try not to smile as she lifts her drink to her lips.

"I have something for you. I think you should look at it." Grayson stands, and starts to walk away, but Maria and I stay where we are. "Jake, you'll want to see this. I'd suggest you follow me."

I look at Maria, and she simply shrugs her shoulders.

"Not my issue." She holds up her drink. "I'm getting drunk and hopefully fucking an Italian stallion. You have fun with your crazy brother."

Shaking my head, I leave her at the bar and follow Grayson out. He makes his way over to a car and goes straight to the trunk, popping it open. When he does, I see Mercedes—the very same man I slit the throat of earlier tonight.

"You forgot to clean up your mess." He nods to Mercedes. "Now, I can take this to the local authorities, or you can give me what I want. I'm only asking for *one woman*... I'm down and desperate."

I grind my teeth as I stare at him, then let out a huff.

"I'm sure they would be happy to search your apartment. I wonder what they would do with your pretty redhead. She was there, right? Probably even has his blood on her."

"You can't have any of them," I tell him. "But Avani is looking to move. I will offer your position to her. She loves sex. And if you pay her right—"

"I'll pay her double what you do," he says. I glance back at the body.

"Burn it."

He smirks before he says, "After I remove the teeth,

of course. Wouldn't want you to go back on your word. I may just hold on to them for a little while, you know, until your debt is paid." He closes the trunk and walks around to the driver's side, getting in and speeding off.

Can I kill my brother?

I should.

CHAPTER 30

Choke me softly

ORIANA

W hen I wake, the sun is shining through the curtains and the smell of food permeates the room. I stretch my arm to the other side of the bed, remembering that I fell asleep with Jake next to me. I reach for the shirt I removed last night, pull it over my head, then step into the main room to find him sitting at the table with a paper in his hands. He's reading and has not even noticed I'm here.

"Eat," he orders.

Okay. Well, maybe he did notice. I take the same seat I had last night. He puts the paper down and stares at me.

"You didn't sleep with me?" I ask, grabbing a piece of bacon.

"No. I figured you wouldn't take too kindly to waking up and being choked again."

"I enjoyed it last night," I purr, and his brow quirks ever so slightly before he turns serious.

"That's because you knew I wouldn't do it to hurt you while I was awake."

"But asleep…"

"I have no control."

We sit in silence until I eat the last of the bacon, then he asks, "Did you want to shop? It's our last day, so you may as well do something you want to do."

"I would love that," I reply as I stand. "I'll get dressed."

"Oriana."

"Yes?" I turn back to face him.

"I plan to fuck you again before we leave."

"Promises, promises," I whisper, just loud enough for him to hear. His chuckle follows me as I go and get changed. Once I slip on a flowy dress with a pair of flat ballerina shoes, I head back to join him.

"You get ready faster than any woman I know," he compliments.

"You make me come faster than any other man has," I say cheekily.

He sucks air through his teeth while he smirks. "And more than once," he adds.

I grin as I reach him, and he puts his hand on the small of my back as we leave.

We're pretty close to everything, so we decide to

walk. He takes me to an area littered with designer shops. Walking into one, he sits on the couch, waiting patiently as I look at the clothing. I'm used to wearing designer dresses—it was expected of me when I was in public with Kyler—but other than that, my closet is full of average brands that make me feel comfortable.

I don't have money to splurge on expensive clothes anymore because I'm saving all my pay to one day buy a place with only my name on it, we had a prenup. The house I shared with Kyler was in his name, not mine. It's part of the reason I was the one who had to walk out. Plus, that house was too big for just the two of us. I'm not sure I could have lived there by myself.

"Oriana." I look over to Jake as the saleslady gives him a glass of wine. "Try that on." He nods to an all-black bodysuit.

"Nice choice, sir," the lady says in English. She pulls it off the rack, takes it to the changing room, and smiles at me.

"I would never wear that," I tell him.

"You would...for me."

"Would I, now?" I smile.

"You try it on. I'll buy whatever it is your heart desires."

"Anything?" I question.

"You can have anything." I nod and step into the changing room. I strip off my dress as it slides onto the floor I reach for my leather body suit and slip it on. This isn't your average leather body suit, though. It has cutouts over the stomach and nipples that are covered in lace. It's a G-string in the back and fits my breasts perfectly. I take a deep breath as I pull back the curtain. The saleslady beams at me. When I look at Jake, he stands and hands her his black credit card.

"Charge me for this and three more in different colors," he says, not taking his eyes off me. "And leave. And don't come back until I call for you."

"That's no way to speak to her," I reprimand.

He turns back to the lady. "Buy yourself something nice as well."

She nods, smiling happily as she spins on her heel, shutting the curtains behind her.

His hand grazes my stomach through the lace before it touches the leather.

"Aren't you going to ask me what I wanted?" I question him as his hand dips lower.

"I'd buy you a fucking country if I get to see you in this every day." His voice drips with lust.

"Well, no need for that, but I would take a kiss."

"That's what you want?" he asks, his fingers halting at my hips.

I nod and stretch up to touch his lips with mine. When he lets me and doesn't pull back, I smile against his lips.

"I like the way you taste," I whisper.

He pushes me back into the changing room and shuts the curtain, matching each step I take until I'm against the wall. "I like the way you taste too. And if you wish to taste me again, I need to taste you first."

"But—"

He cuts me off by slipping a finger under the leather and straight into me. I gasp as he pushes it in, and he smirks, clearly enjoying watching me come undone right in front of him. "Already so wet. Now we definitely have to buy it."

I bite my lip as his thumb sweeps across my clit. And just as I start moving on him, it's gone, and his fingers are now out of me and in his mouth.

"You can take your payment now." He grins mischievously.

I lean forward and waste no time raising up on my tip-toes and planting my lips straight on his again.

The world disappears.

And all I can see, hear, and breathe is him.

Before him, I would never be caught doing what we just did. He makes me feel alive like I am worth so much more than arm candy.

I'm afraid to say it, but I think I am falling in love with a man who isn't my husband.

"Sir." He slides his teeth over my tongue as he pulls away, breaks our kiss, and steps out of the changing room. "I'm sorry to interrupt, sir, but I wanted to show you this. Thought it may interest you as well."

I slide on my dress after I take off the leather. When I pull the curtain open, I see Jake holding another leather item and I peer over his shoulder to view it.

"What is it?" I ask.

"Restraints." He smiles. "To match your new outfit." He hands them back to the lady. "Add it to my bill."

I blush as she walks away.

"Now, let's finish shopping, then we'll go eat."

We leave the shop hand in hand, and he doesn't complain once when I drag him in and out of other stores.

I tried to pay for everything, but when I got back to the hotel that night and checked my account, I found that not once had my card been charged.

———

THAT SAME DAY, we leave and head back home.

After we land, we get in his car, and he takes me home. When we pull up, I see Harvey and Simone sitting outside and they're yelling at each other.

Simone drops her face to her hands, and Harvey looks pained.

"You can still escape. They haven't seen you yet," Jake says.

"No, it's late. I need sleep. I have work tomorrow."

"You could stay at mine," he offers.

His.

I have no idea where Jake even lives. I've only ever been to his bars and sex club.

"What are we?" I ask. "I mean...I only ask because you're inviting me back to your place, and you didn't answer me when I asked last time." My body turns, and I give him my full attention, forgetting about my brother and Simone for the moment.

"I don't like labels. Besides, have labels ever served you well?" he asks.

"Okay, no labels," I agree, then turn to open the door.

Jake stops me with a hand on my shoulder. "You're mad."

My tongue slides over my teeth as I try to think of the correct response to give him. "Not mad, just confused."

"We've known each other for a few months, Oriana. We've been having fun. Dare I say, more fun than I have had with anyone in my life. So why do we have to label it?"

"Because I'm not someone who just casually sleeps

around. I do relationships. And this..." I wave between us, "is confusing to me."

"My intention is to not confuse you, you know that."

"Do I?" I ask as a knock comes on the window. I look up to see Simone and I unlock the door. "I have to go."

"Get divorced first, Oriana. Then we can talk."

"I've been trying," I say with a huff as I step out of the car.

The driver already has my bags out and on the steps of my house. He goes back to the car, and I watch as they drive off.

Turning back to Simone, I see my brother is no longer there.

"What's going on?" I ask.

Her eyes flick to the door, which is where I'm guessing Harvey went, and then to the ground.

"I'm pregnant," she says quietly.

Oh, wow. Did not expect that answer.

"Is it..." I don't know how to ask.

"Yes, it's Harvey's." She raises her gaze to mine. "I just told him, and he didn't take it well."

No, I'm guessing he wouldn't have. Harvey travels a lot, it's what he does. Having a baby would change that, would change *him*. I don't know how he will react, but I do know he would be a good father.

"I'm sure you two can sort it out," I try to reassure her.

"Yeah, I don't know about that. I mean, I had hoped so. But I'm not really sure now." She shrugs. "It's new. I only found out this morning, and when he sent me a text telling me he was home, I knew I had to tell him."

"Do you actually want children?" I ask. I have never really asked her that question before, as I've never seen her in a fully committed relationship, and she had voiced her dislike for children but I guess this changes things.

"I didn't think I did, but now things are different."

"Do you love Harvey?"

"I do. Is that crazy?" she whispers. "I mean, I think he just thinks of me as a fling. But I don't see us as a fling at all."

"Do you want to come in?" I ask, nodding to the door.

"I don't think he wants me in there right now," she says in a broken whisper.

"Do you want me to come with you? I just need to put my bags away, and I'm all yours," I offer.

"No, it's okay. I might just curl up and watch a movie and pass out."

I place my hand on her shoulder. "I can talk to him. Do you want me to?"

"He's your brother first, O. Maybe he needs your support."

"And you are my best friend, so I can give it to you as well."

"Simone." We both look to the house as Harvey calls her name. "Come inside." He holds open the door.

"I'm giving you your space, Harvey. You need space and time."

"Get inside, Simone," he says, but even though it sounds like an order he said it gently. I stand there as she makes her way up the stairs, and the minute she reaches him, he cups her face, leans down, and kisses her lips softly. "It was just a lot. I'm sorry."

She nods and kisses him back. "It's a lot for me too." Tears run down her cheeks, and he wipes them away.

"I get that, I do. I had to process." His hands fall from her face, and he guides her inside. Over his shoulder, he says to me, "Welcome back, stoner." He winks, and I give him my best eye roll. Simone laughs as I grab my bag and head inside. I smile fondly as they both disappear into his room, then I go straight to mine.

I think I need to find somewhere else to live.

I mean, I don't think my brother would kick me out, but if he's having a baby with my best friend, I highly doubt they will want me in their space.

Unpacking my bag, I see the bags of clothes Jake bought me, and I smile as I pull out the leather body-suit and remember what I had to do to get that kiss.

Would I do it again? That's a hell yes. Any day of the week.

That man may hate to be kissed or give kisses, but I cherish every single one I've had with him.

And I will take, and take, until I can no longer take any more.

CHAPTER 31

She was already mine

JAKE

"You won." I lean against the wall outside of my club as Kyler stands there with two body-guards flanking him. It's late, but obviously he had something he needed to say to me that couldn't wait.

"I always win," I remind him.

He bites back a remark as someone walks past us. Wouldn't want to ruin his reputation. When it's all clear he says, "I've signed the papers. She's all yours."

"The moment my hands touched her, she was mine," I state.

"Yeah, but one day soon, she will wake up and realize what a mistake that was," he barks, smiling. "She likes to be good, it's her personality, and you are anything but. You run a sex club... I know for sure she won't want to be associated with that."

"I fucked her in my office at the sex club," I taunt.

"She liked it, a lot, in case you were wondering." I step closer to him. "You may think she is this perfect little thing, but I want to tell you, that was the box *you* put her in. She is anything but, and trust me, I know because I'm surrounded by women every day. She may be perfect with her mouth..." I smile cruelly, "but her actions when you make her come are not that of a good girl."

"She was my wife," he snarls, and his bodyguards step in to stop him from doing anything stupid, but I don't even flinch.

"And now she is my whore," I tell him. "It seems you didn't know what was good for you. But one person's trash is always someone else's treasure."

A smirk slips across his lips before he spins and walks away. When I turn around, Avani is standing at the door with her arms crossed over one another.

"You gave me away?" she asks, pouting. "You don't want me to work for you anymore?"

"You were leaving, Avani. Did you forget?" I stalk past her and down the stairs. The door shuts behind us, and I hear her heels clicking as she follows me.

"That's beside the point," she replies.

"I told him it was your choice, so did you choose?" I step behind the bar to collect the earnings from tonight's clients.. When I face her again, she flicks her hair over her shoulder.

"I did."

"And do you plan to leave me in suspense?" I push.

"Why did you pick me?" she asks.

"Because I know you can handle yourself," I tell her truthfully.

"Well, yeah, of course I can." She smiles. "He's hot, you know. Your brother."

"He won't buy you Gucci bags, Avani," I scoff.

"Of course he will. I requested one for every month I'm there. I learned a thing or two from you, you know. How to get exactly what I want." She winks.

"So you took him up on his offer?"

She places her hands on her hips and replies, "I did."

"See? It works out for both of us." I smile at her. "I'll give you a nice bonus for your time with me, and you know you are always welcome back."

She takes a seat at the bar.

"It's okay to love her, you know," she says. "The redhead. I see how you are with her. You were always fixated on work, but with her—"

"What?" My forehead wrinkles in confusion.

"You're fixated on her instead, and it's nice. I hope one day to have a man look at me the same way you look at her if I'm comfortable enough to get into that situation." She shrugs her shoulders. "All I'm saying is, it seems you chose well." With that, she gets up and leaves, and I stand there contemplating her words.

If you had asked me a year ago if something other then my work would be on my mind, I would tell you no. Work is what has driven me for as long as I can remember, yet all I can think about lately is a little redhead who doesn't know how to say fuck.

The day I killed my stepfather wasn't planned, it just kind of happened. I was older, and I wasn't going to continue taking his shit, no matter how much my mother pleaded his case. I didn't expect to take his life that day. I just wanted to beat him real good, so he understood exactly what it was like to wake up the same way he woke me up for years on end.

My mother was on nightshift because she always worked while he sat on his fucking ass and drank whatever he could get his hands on. He used her like a toy as if she were a puppet for his imagination.

I went to my bedroom and shut the door like I normally would, but I couldn't lock it since he removed the lock when I was younger.

On Friday nights, he would always pass out in his recliner before he would wake and visit my room, so I knew it was the perfect time to show him that he could no longer do what he was doing to me.

When I heard something drop from my bedroom, I got up and crept out of the room to see him in the recliner, lounged back and fast asleep. The remote had fallen to the floor and the bottle he was drinking from dangled loosely from his hand. I wasn't one hundred percent sure what I intended to do, but I knew now was the only time I could do it.

When I stood over him, and he didn't move, I leaned forward and placed both my hands around his neck, and started to squeeze. He woke, his eyes blood-shot from either lack of sleep or the alcohol. I wasn't sure which. Nor did I care. His hands clawed at mine the same way mine had his countless nights when he would visit me in my room.

There were days that he would beat me so badly my mother would tell me not to go to school and to sit in the backyard where he couldn't see me. It was hard covering bruises around the neck, and sometimes teachers asked questions. But I didn't really answer them, and I guess they weren't paid enough to care.

He tried to punch me, but the thing is, when you've been punched so many times by the same person, you become numb to it after a while.

I intended to let go. I really, really did. But the look in his eyes told me that he was going to make me pay for my insolence, and I knew that couldn't happen. So I applied more pressure, blocking his windpipe. His fingers dug deeper into my arms, trying to dislodge me, but he was drunk, and I was dead sober. He couldn't beat me this time, no matter how hard he tried.

I remember the smile that touched my lips as I watched him pass out from the lack of oxygen and how my hands wouldn't release their grip.

My mother came home that night, or maybe it was the next morning—I kind of lost track of time—to find him in the recliner, not breathing, and me on the floor just watching him, waiting for him to jump up.

In my mother's eyes, all I saw was the relief wash over her face.

She went to prison for his murder in my place. It was the only act of love I ever remember her showing me. I haven't seen her since that day and, to be honest, I never intend to see her again.

I wonder if that's why I'm so attracted to Oriana. Her composure, her sweetness, they're just not something I've ever dealt with before.

And I quite like how that feels.

To have someone so kind.

Gentle.

Demure.

Actually, I quite like her.

CHAPTER 32

I'll be a possession for great sex, thank you very much

ORIANA

K yler is at my door.

I'm taken aback by seeing him again.

He looks good, but then again, he always does. Looks have never been an issue for Kyler. It's his personality not quite meshing with mine that was the problem.

He hands me a stack of papers. When I scan the first page, I recognize the divorce paperwork.

"You asked for nothing?" he questions as if surprised.

"It's all yours," I answer.

Kyler slides his hands into his pockets at my words.

"I was a bad husband. I'm not even going to deny that. But you were a good wife." I go to speak, but he holds up his hand. "Let me finish." I nod for him to go on. "I cheated on you not just emotionally but physically. I'm not sure why I did it, but I figured you should know."

His admission shocks and hurts me all at once.

Oh my gosh, that hurts.

It really stings.

I clutch my chest and feel a tear leave my eye.

I've asked him this before, and he lied. *Was everything just a lie?*

"I gave you the Hamptons house, Oriana. You worked for it. It's yours."

I can't respond. How can he just drop a bomb like that and expect me to what? Say thank you?

Was our marriage only sacred to me?

"Jake only sees you as one of his possessions, you know that, right?" he says, then pulls out his phone and pushes play on a recording.

And I hear Jake's voice.

"And now she is my whore. It seems you didn't know what was good for you. But one person's trash is always someone else's treasure."

When I meet Kyler's expression, I see him smiling.

"And this pleases you?" I ask incredulously upon hearing another man call me trash. How can that put a smile on his face. At least I know the reason Jake would have said it is because he was taunting Kyler, I am not stupid. But Jake has shown me more of everything in the short time I've known him than my husband ever did for our entire marriage.

"I just thought you should know." He shrugs.

"So what? I'll leave him?" I shake my head. "That's not going to happen either. I'm happy with him. Why does that make you so mad when you were sleeping with other women? Why does it even bother you?" I ask, growing more frustrated by the second. "Actually, you know what? You should leave. I think that would be for the best. Just. Leave." I step back inside and try to shut the door, but he holds it open with his hand.

"I'm sorry, Oriana."

"You should be," I seethe, then I push harder, and the door finally closes.

"Oriana." I turn around to see Simone standing there, shock written all over her face. She wraps her arms around me, and then my brother does the same from behind. I'm lucky to have these people in my life, there are not many people who can say the same. Like those women Jake helps. They don't have that luxury. Their only luxury is him, and I guess despite how bad it sounds, all his women who I have met seem to be happy. It could be an illusion, but I'm not so sure.

"I'm okay. I promise I'm good," I tell them as they let me go. "He gave me the Hamptons house."

"Wow, okay," Harvey says, surprised but still looks at me with worry.

"I'm going to sell it and buy myself something small and donate the rest."

"That sounds like a wonderful idea." Simone beams, her smile wide.

"You don't have to move out. I like having you here," Harvey says.

I lay my hand on Simone's arm and look at my brother. "You're going to be a father soon, so I think it's time I move out." I smile, and I mean it. It's time for me to stand on my own two feet. "But thank you for letting me stay here."

"What are brothers for?" He grins as he ruffles my hair as if I am still a child.

I'VE COME to realize that my relationship with Jake is not co-dependent. I was very co-dependent with Kyler. Everything I did, everywhere I went, I had to think of how *he* would react. Jake gives me my freedom, even though technically, I guess we never put a label on our relationship. It's nice to know if I need him, he would come.

I sent the revised divorce paperwork to the lawyer, so very soon, I'll officially be single. The media has already gotten wind of our divorce, and Kyler's face is all over the news and social media, saying that he is now a bachelor. Maybe Kyler will be happier single, being able to do whatever it is he pleases. I think that's what he always wanted right from the beginning.

I push through the coffee shop door, walk to the counter, and order my matcha tea.. As I wait, I hear my name being called from behind. When I turn around, I see someone I was hoping never to see again.

"It's Sailor. Do you remember me? You're Jake's girl, right? You came to my house for my anniversary." I give her a strained smile as my name is called for my order. "Do you have time to join me? I hardly get alone time these days, and some girl talk would be amazing."

Do I say no?

Is that an appropriate thing to say to the wife of a mafia boss?

"Are you okay?" She lays a hand on my shoulder. I glance at her hand, and she quickly removes it. "Sorry, did I do something to offend you?" I lift my eyes and see a few people staring at us.

"I know who your family is... Who your husband is."

"Well, I had hoped so..." She sounds confused. "I mean, you did come to my house."

"I didn't know then," I add.

"Oh, I see..." Understanding lights her expression. "I didn't know who he was either when I met him.

Actually, *when he took me* would be a more accurate way to say it, I guess."

"Took you?" I question, eyes widening.

"Yep, right from that club of Jake's. My ex-husband—may his lying, cheating ass rest in peace—gave me to him like a piece of meat." I flinch at her words, but she brushes it off. "He's a good man. To me, at least." She smiles fondly. "My husband is rough around the edges but he's good."

"I'm happy for you."

"Please don't be afraid. I just wanted you to know that I get the scared part, but we are all good. I swear."

I want to believe her, but I'm not sure how to. I guess the same could be said for Jake. In other people's books, he may be considered downright awful, but in mine, he isn't.

"Can I ask you what your plans are for today?" Sailor asks.

"I have a house I need to sell."

Sailor claps her hands.

"Oh, what house? I used to be a real estate agent."

"Really," I reply as we take a seat. I grab my phone and pull up the photographs of the house and show them to Sailor.

"Is that in The Hamptons?" she asks, and I reply, "Yes."

"Sold. I want it."

Did she seriously just offer to buy my house? To say I'm surprised would be an understatement.

"I'll give you above the asking price." She sips on her coffee like she just offered to buy my old used purse instead.

"Do you not want to talk to your husband about that first?" I ask.

"No. Good Lord, no. Sometimes he has more money than sense. I'll buy it and surprise him."

"And he'll be okay with that?"

"Who cares? I'll give him sex, and he will forgive me. Or I'll show him my boobs and get the same result. Either way works." She shrugs, and I huff out a laugh. *I guess she knows how to get what she wants.*

Her phone starts ringing, and she excuses herself to answer it. I drink my tea and wonder if she is being serious.

Did she just buy my house over tea?

"Adora needs my help at her store, so I have to run. But please call me. I do want that house. I'm not joking." She passes me her phone. "Add your number so I can call you later."

So I add my number and hand the phone back, then she waves as she strolls out the door.

I get my phone out and message Jake.

Me: Did I tell you the divorce papers are signed and sent?

I WAIT for a response but get nothing.

When I arrive home, I find Jake waiting for me. He's sitting on the step, his face propped on his hands, with a far-off expression on his face.

"Divorce? Hey..." When he finally notices me and raises his head, I can see the strain in his dark gray eyes, but there's something else there too.

Something painful, almost.

I sit next to him and put my bag to the side as I reach out and touch his leg. "Yep..." I pause, searching his face. "Are you okay?"

"Do you want to marry me?" he asks.

I'm so taken aback by his question that I snatch my hand away and immediately raise it to my hair.

He grips it, stopping me. "You do that when you're nervous. Am I making you nervous?" Jake asks, sliding his hand into mine and lacing our fingers together.

"Tell me what's really bothering you," I say, ignoring his question about marriage.

He sighs, then says, "My mother showed up."

"And that's a problem because?" I ask, confused.

He doesn't really tell me personal things so I am in the dark right now.

"Because she is no longer in prison for the murder of my stepfather, and she is asking for a relationship with me."

"She killed him?" I thought Jake said he killed him.

"No, I did." He doesn't let go of my hand when I try to pull away, just holds it tighter.

"The therapist suggested I share more with you. Would you like to go to my place?"

Therapist? He's seeing a therapist to be better, for me?

"Umm..." I don't know what to say. I mean, a part of me wants to go with him, but the other part is shocked.

I wanted this, didn't I? For Jake to share more of himself with me.

It's a big thing for him, and he's shared before that no one really knows him. But he keeps on giving me tiny snippets of him, and I take them willingly.

"I invited her for dinner tomorrow night. I would like it if you would attend," he states.

"Tomorrow works fine," I reply. At least then, it gives me time to think more.

"Divorced," he says like he can't believe it. "I'm going to marry you one day soon." He beams at me as he stands. "I'm not sure of many things, but of that, I am positive."

"Marry me?" I choke out, wondering why that doesn't scare me more after just ending one disastrous marriage.

"Yep." He leans in and lifts my chin until our lips are close to each other. "And I'm going to make you scream every bad word possible when I make you come."

"You tried that, it doesn't work."

"I can always fuck it out of you." He winks before his lips touch mine. He kisses me softly, sliding his tongue past my lips and tasting me. His kisses are like bliss. They take over your body and send sparks into every follicle of my being making me want to combust. I close my eyes before he pulls away abruptly. "I like you, Oriana."

"I like you too, Jake."

"Good." He turns, walks to his car, and opens the door. "Go inside, so I know you are safe."

I stand from the steps and turn to go in, my knees a little wobblily from that toe curling kiss. But before I open the door, I blurt out, "Kyler recorded you the other day..." I turn my head to catch his reaction, "when you said I was your whore."

"I know."

"You think of me like that?" I ask, a little angry.

"Of course I do. You're also so much more. But he isn't privileged enough to know that. Only you are." He winks, then adds, "I can be your whore any time you please."

"I may like that very much." My lips pull up to a smile at his words. *Is Jake romantic?* Because that to me is super romantic. Maybe he has warped my head, but I am here for it. All of it.

"That's my girl," he says, then waves his hand. "Now, get that sweet ass inside before I decide to change my mind and come up and tie you to your bed and fuck the whore right into you."

I'm giggling as I reach the door.

"Promises, promises," I sing back to him. When I step in and turn back to him, I see the smile that was missing when he first arrived, and it looks good on him. "You'll pick me up tomorrow?"

"Of course."

"How should I dress?"

His eyes roam me. "I prefer you in your birthday suit." His tongue darts out and licks his lips. "But I guess any type of clothes will do."

"Clothes I can do." I nod. "Goodnight, Jake."

"Goodnight, Oriana. Dream of me?"

"Of course." I shut the door and lean against it. *Did he really just ask me to marry him? Or was I dreaming?*

CHAPTER 33

He's rich, let's fuck

JAKE

Oriana sits in my car, staring up at my house.

"I didn't expect..." She trails off as she turns her head toward me. "I mean, I knew you had money."

"Is it not to your liking?" I ask.

"I think it's to everyone's liking." A smile touches her lips. "The drive doesn't bother you? You work in the city, and this is kind of far from the city."

My eyes scan the area, flitting over my stable, which has three horses, and the chickens in their pen.

"My office has a bed when I'm too tired to drive," I explain. "But this? This is my home."

A car pulls up behind us, and I don't even need to look back to know it's my mother. Oriana places her hand in mine and gives me a squeeze. How did she know that simple touch was all I needed?

"Are you sure you want me to meet her? You can change your mind if it's too much," Oriana states with so much compassion in her gorgeous green eyes that, for some reason, it gives me goose bumps. Then I look in the rearview mirror and cringe. My mother is out of her car and standing there, her eyes locked on the house.

"I want you here. You are the only person in the world I want here at this very moment." She leans in and her lips touch mine, soft and pure.

I'm not even sure how I managed to get her.

But you can bet I will do anything to keep her.

Oriana is now mine, and no one will take her from me.

No matter what!

"We should get out," she whispers, her lips still on mine. "Your mother is waiting." She pulls away, and a small sigh leaves me as she is the first to get out of the car. I wait a second, catch my breath, then follow Oriana out of the car.

What will my mother say?

More importantly, what does she want?

After all this time with no contact, I know she has to want something.

Oriana walks over to my mother and offers her hand to introduce herself.

"Are you his wife, or—"

"One day, she will be my wife," I say, stepping up next to Oriana and placing my hand on the small of her back. Oriana says nothing, just smiles at my mother. "Mother, it's been a long time."

Her eyes scan me.

"You look good. And you've done well for yourself, I see." Her gaze once again goes to my house. "Despite everything."

"You mean despite your husband beating me every night."

She flinches at my words but says nothing in return.

"How long have you been out?" Oriana asks, changing the subject.

My mother's eyes flick to mine, and I say, "Oriana knows everything."

"A few months. I got a job at a small café, cleaning. I wanted to get presentable before I found Jake."

"You look great," Oriana replies.

I have to admit Mom does look good. She appears so much better than I remember. Maybe that's what being sober does to someone.

"Is it okay that I'm here?" Mom asks me nervously.

"Oriana, this is Samantha, my mother." I realize I never introduced them and continue with, "Let's go inside before I change my mind." I move to head inside but reach back and grab Oriana's hand, pulling her along with me.

"What are we eating?" Oriana asks.

"The cook has made something."

"You have a cook?" Oriana whispers. "Lord..."

I chuckle at her attempt to swear.

Pushing open the door, I lead the way in. Oriana gapes when we pass through the large foyer on the way to the dining area.

"This is beautiful," she whispers when she sees the large, circular wooden table with blue velvet chairs.

"Sit." I sweep my arm toward the table and they each take a seat, my mother sitting closer to Oriana than me, which is fine. I choose the seat on the other side of Oriana as the cook brings out a platter of cheese and places it in front of us.

"Jake, can you tell me what you do? Are you a bar owner?" my mother asks.

Oriana reaches for some cheese and waits for me to answer, but I'm fixated on that cube of cheese in her hand as she brings it to her mouth.

I know something that will fit in her mouth—just barely. I chuckle to myself about my lewd thought.

"I own several bars, even a sex club."

My mother's eyes go wide. "Sex club?" she asks, and the surprise in her tone is not lost on me.

"It's not what you think. It's tastefully run," Oriana says, then adds, "Jake is very good at business."

No longer able to hold it in and needing to know, I ask, "Why did you take the fall for me? I was ready to go to jail with a smile on my face at the thought I killed that bastard."

She places her hands flat on the table and takes a steadying breath before replying, "Because I let it happen. It was my fault. I knew it at the time. I would wake to hear you screaming in the middle of the night. And I was too afraid to do anything. He would beat me if I interfered. So—"

"You took the fall in hopes I would forgive you?"

"No. I have never thought you will forgive me, but that doesn't mean I am not going to try for forgiveness."

"The first time I fell asleep with someone next to me, I strangled them," I tell her. My mother's eyes flick to Oriana's neck, but her bruises are gone. Thank fuck.

"You hurt her?" she whispers.

"Not on purpose," Oriana interjects. "He would never hurt me on purpose." Oriana's hand slides under the table and onto my thigh, giving it a squeeze.

"I am this way because of *you*. And I hate *you* because of it," I tell her truthfully. Oriana squeezes my thigh again. My mother looks away, her eyes filling with tears and then one overflows and runs down her cheek. "But I'm learning forgiveness... It's a process."

Mom wipes her eyes and smiles. "I hope I can join that list one day," she says sincerely.

"I'm sure you do," I add.

"Do you know Jake's brother?" Oriana asks, changing the subject.

"Grayson is back?"

"No, he just came to stir up shit. He's just like our father," I say, making light of it.

"You are actually more like him in looks," my mother adds. "I heard your father died. Did you attend his funeral?"

"No, why would I? I didn't attend your husband's either for obvious reasons."

Mom goes silent at my words as the cook brings out our dinner.

We spend the rest of the evening listening to Oriana talk about her new job.

And when my mother leaves...

I plan to fuck my woman.

CHAPTER 34

How I met your mother

ORIANA

"He's very taken with you," Jake's mother says as we walk to her car.

Jake has gone back inside to grab me a jacket because it's getting colder at night. I don't respond to her comment about us because I still don't know where I stand with Jake.

"Just be careful of Grayson. He was always jealous of Jake." Again, I say nothing. "You must think I'm an awful person." Her eyes dip down to the ground. "That I let all that happen under my roof."

"I'm sure you had your reasons."

She meets my gaze and wipes a tear from her eye. "I was struggling, and sometimes when a woman is struggling, she will do anything to survive."

From behind a jacket is placed over my shoulders,

and Jake slides his hand under the fabric to my lower back.

"I hope to see you again...if you would like that?" she asks. He doesn't respond right away, and she pushes for an answer. "Jake?"

He's studying her, an intense expression on his face before he says, "I don't know if I'm ready for that."

"Okay. I'll give you all the time you need." She turns to me. "It was lovely meeting you."

"You too." I smile.

His mother gives Jake one last look before she walks to her car and gets in. We stand there until her taillights are out of sight and it's just us standing in the dark.

"I want you to stay the night in my bed," he rumbles. I give him a curious look. "The therapist suggested it, and I wouldn't have said anything if I thought I could hurt you again."

"If you think—"

His finger against my lip silences me. "I don't think... I know I won't. What happened to me doesn't haunt me anymore." He pauses, swallowing roughly. "What I did to you haunts me." His finger leaves my lip. "I would never hurt you again. Do you get that?"

I can only nod in understanding because I have no idea how he knows that to be true, but I want more than anything to believe him—to believe in him.

It doesn't take Jake long to turn me around and lead me back to the house. His hand doesn't move an inch as we walk the stairs, and he shuts the door behind us.

My feelings for Jake are real and nothing like what I felt for Kyler. I've come to accept that, knowing they are two entirely different people and that not everyone loves the same. I loved Kyler in a way I thought he needed to be loved, but I'm falling in love with Jake in a way that *I need* to be loved.

And I think that's okay.

Jake removes the jacket from my shoulders ever so slowly. He does it with intention, his fingers dragging along my skin and sending goosebumps everywhere. When the jacket falls to the floor, his hands scoop underneath my ass, and he lifts me until my legs wrap around his waist. Then he strides up the stairs with purpose, pushes the bedroom door open with his shoulder and walks in.

That's when I take in the space around me. This is a simple bedroom design for a house that's so grand on the outside. It has no television and no dressers or nightstands. The only thing it contains is a bed and two closed doors, which I can only guess are a closet and bathroom.

"I need my mind silenced at night. So I have to have nothing distracting me from getting a good sleep." I didn't ask for an explanation for his lack of décor, but he gave me one anyway.

When I turn my head toward him, he gives my ass a little squeeze, leans in, then rubs his nose against mine softly. "I want to devour you," he whispers. "Taste every inch of you and let you know that you are mine."

I don't object to his words. Instead, I relish in them.

Jake places me down, then goes to the closet, flicks on the light, and removes his shirt. When he comes back out in just pants, I ogle him as he adjusts himself.

He takes a moment to look me up and down before he says, "I think you should remove *everything*."

"You do, do you?" I reply coyly. "And why is that?" I lift my hand to my shirt but don't remove it.

"Because I plan to fuck you so hard that the words that leave your mouth will be filthy." He sucks air through his teeth, and his stare eats me alive. "I *will* make you swear. I *will* make sure you bring every bad word in your vocabulary out when I'm inside of you."

"That won't happen," I tell him.

"Oh, but I think it very much will." He prowls closer, like an animal on the hunt, and starts to circle me. "Remove the pants first," he orders and slaps my ass, hard, making me gasp.

I flick the buttons and bend over as I drop them to the floor. I'm wearing a red, lacy G-string underneath.

He groans as I remain bent over in front of him, and I take my time as I stand. When I look over my shoulder at him, his eyes are glued to my ass.

"That was naughty," he scolds.

I shrug, and he slaps my ass again, harder than before. I yelp but don't move away.

"My handprint on your ass is my new favorite thing." I go to remove my shirt, but he pulls my hand down. "Stop." He leans in from behind, his cock straining in his pants as he pushes it against my ass. "Now, spread them and touch your toes."

I widen my stance a little and do as he says. When my hands touch my toes, I hear a soft vibrating sound before something touches me through my G-string and moves up to my clit. Releasing a moan, I raise my head to see he has a small purple vibrator he's using on me.

He lifts my G-string and slides the device inside. I hear his groan of pleasure as I spread my legs a little wider. Then he moves the vibrator to the perfect rhythm, back and forth, all over my clit. I feel myself getting wet, really wet, before I feel something warm. My eyes closed at one point, and now I open them to see his mouth at my opening, the vibrator still buzzing against my clit.

How is this so pleasurable?

Why do I want to slide his face up and down me until I am screaming?

Just as my hips start to move, his face and the vibrator disappear. And I'm left hanging upside down and wanting friction.

"Stand," he barks, and I quickly react. "You can remove your shirt now." I whip the material over my head to find he is now in front of me. He motions to my bra, indicating that should go next, so I unclasp it and drop it to the floor, leaving me dressed in my soaked G-string.

The vibrator in his hand has been replaced with something that is silver in color. "Close your eyes," he whispers. When my eyes fall shut, I feel pressure on my right nipple, followed by the left. Something tugs on both at the same time, and I open my eyes to see a chain between my breasts, connected by a clamp on each nipple.

"What is..." I can't think of the words. "What is that?"

He doesn't answer. Instead, he tugs on the chain a little, and I bite back a moan. His smirk is on full display when my eyes lift to his face.

"That's my girl," he croons, leaning in and biting my bottom lip, tasting it as he does, before releasing it with a pop.

His hand slides between us and finds my clit again,

rubbing it, while his other hand tugs the chain between my breasts. And I feel it...*everywhere.*

I can feel my orgasm getting close.

And then it gets taken away.

He stops.

Leans in and kisses me, telling me to keep my hands at my sides.

Then he does the same thing over and over again.

I count three times, three kisses, and on the last one, I'm so frustrated that all I want to do is strangle him.

He chuckles at my aggression and steps away.

I watch as he drops his pants, his hard penis coming into view, the piercing wet with his pre-cum. His hand covers it, and he strokes up and down. I lick my lips at the show he's giving me.

"Tell me what I want to hear," he orders, while I stand there, mesmerized by the movement of his hand. "Oriana," he snaps, then makes a motion with two fingers, pointing to my eyes and then his. "Eyes on mine."

"What?" I ask. I start fidgeting because I can literally feel my wetness leaking down my legs.

"Repeat after me...." He smirks. "Jake, I want you to bend me over that bed and fuck me until I'm seeing stars, so much so that my sweet, sweet cunt is throbbing for more." My eyes go wide at his words, and he steps closer to me, leaning in, his breath coasting over my lips. "You can never talk like that to anyone else but me, do you understand?"

I know he means the context, but I am shocked anyway.

I don't know why I never liked swearing. Maybe it's because when I was younger, my grandparents would tell me how a lady should never cuss.

I seemed to be the only person I knew who didn't swear.

It wasn't an issue to some.

Others found it weird.

My parents loved that I was a lady.

Jake? Well, Jake wants those words to be saved only for him.

Too lost in my head, I forget about the clamps until he pulls them, making my eyes bounce to find his.

"I'm waiting." He growls impatiently, then slaps my ass and pulls me in close, my body now pressed against his, my hardened nipples brushing against his chest, and our bodies taut with lust.

"That mouth isn't dirty..." He smirks when I press my hips forward. "Yet."

"I..."

He pushes in closer so I can feel him against my clit, and I lick my lips.

"Jake."

"Hmm..." he hums, his eyes fixed on my breasts.

"I want you to fuck me now."

His body stills.

His eyes, so dangerous, find mine.

"Fuck. I think I might come with your words alone." I can't help the small giggle that leaves me. "Tell me... how do you want it," he says, his mouth finding my neck. "Nice and slow..." he kisses his way down, "or rough?"

"Both. Just *please* fuck me." That word feels good to say to him. Only him, though. I would never say that to any other person in my life.

He pulls away and steps back. As he does, I remove the panties and wait for his instruction.

"Turn around, place your hands on the bed, and spread your legs." I get into position without asking any questions. Jake comes up behind me, and his hand trails down my back before it stops on my ass. I feel him tease my entrance. "Rough," he says and before I can say anything, he also whispers, "Gentle." And then he slides straight into me. His hands find my hair, and he curls it around his fist, pulling my head back as he slides in and out.

"Tell me, do you want me to fuck you faster or slower?" he asks firmly.

"Slower," I whisper.

He slows his thrusts and ever so gently pulls all the way out of me. I feel the loss straight away and go to turn my head, but he grips my hair tighter.

"Say it," he whispers, his cock returning and teasing me again. "Say it, Oriana."

"Fuck me," I murmur.

"That's my girl." He moans before he slides straight back in.

He fucks me until I see stars, and when I think I can't possibly stand a second longer, he makes me come. Then he flips me over, slides straight back into me, and lifts my legs over his shoulders.

This time he goes slow, his fingers finding my mouth and sliding over my lips, as he takes me in.

"You are mine. You get that, right?" Unable to speak, I simply nod. "Good. Now let me show this cunt how much I love it." He pulls out, backs away a few inches, then leans down and places his mouth on my clit. My flesh is sore and hypersensitive, but he shows it the respect it deserves and tastes it so tenderly.

I'm lost in him.

And at the end, when I'm delirious...

I think I even agreed to marry him.

CHAPTER 35

I love you, equal sex?

JAKE

I wake with a start.

When I turn to see Oriana peacefully lying next to me, a part of my soul sings with happiness it's never experienced before.

Who would have thought that the woman I saw walking down the aisle to another man would one day be mine?

Because that's what she is.

Mine.

I place my hand just above her mouth to check that she's still breathing. Sighing in relief, I get up. She moans as I move but rolls over onto her bare stomach and goes back to sleep.

I start pacing in the room.

My therapist explained that this would be a big step.

That seeing her here, in my space, would help me.

She would be a fixture.

Now, the thing is, how do I convince her to never leave?

I asked her to marry me again.

She agreed. Though, I doubt she remembers.

I want her to be in my house, in my bed, with my ring on her finger.

That's how I see her.

And that's not something I ever envisioned for myself.

If you had asked me a year ago if this was at all possible, I would have laughed and told you to fuck off.

But one bad night for her turned my life on its ass.

To her, that night will always be tainted with bad memories, which just shows how strong and resilient she is that she has overcome them.

And for me...

It brought me her.

The one woman I would give anything.

"Jake." I turn to see her peering at me. "Are you okay?"

"I didn't hurt you," I say, my tone full of awe.

"I know, Jake." Her voice is soft.

"How could you trust I wouldn't hurt you?" I ask, walking over to the bed.

She turns and sits back against the headboard, pulling the sheet up to cover her breasts. Not sure why, as they are one of my favorite things to look at, other than her smile, of course.

"I'm really not sure how to describe it," she starts, those rainforest eyes locking with mine, warming me from the inside. "But I wanted to have faith in you, and I'm glad I did." She beams and that smile lights her eyes. "Now, come back to bed. I need to sleep for the next few hours."

My phone starts ringing, but I ignore it. It keeps on ringing as I climb in next to her.

"Answer it. I'm not going anywhere."

"Move in with me?" I ask.

"One day, maybe." She winks, then lays her head on my chest. "Let's wait until we hit the six-month mark at least, then ask me again."

"That's unfair. I wanted you from the minute I saw you," I argue. "And I have a feeling I've loved you from the minute I saw you as well."

Her eyes find mine from my chest, and her hand touches my heart as she looks up at me. "You love me?" she asks, her voice low, unsure.

"Fucking oath I do. But that one moment in time where I hurt you, with my very own hands, I knew then that I could not live without you. I knew I had to fight myself to believe it, and now you," I say, reaching for my phone as it rings again.

This time I answer, and my brother's voice comes through, not giving her a chance to respond.

"I love you too," Oriana whispers before she kisses my chest and lays back down on it.

"Sooo..." he draws out the word before continuing, "I may have killed Avani."

"What?" I bark, confused.

"Or I'm going to kill him," Avani screams in the background. "He's trying to fuck my roommate," she says loudly. "My roommate, Jake. Tell your brother to knock it off, or I'll *end him*."

"Is this a joke? Fuck off," I growl angrily, and then hang up.

Oriana giggles next to me.

ONE MONTH LATER...

"YOU SHOULDN'T BUY IT," I tell Oriana as we pull up to an apartment she has been looking at. Keir and Sailor bought her property in the Hamptons, and she is planning to buy her own place.

"Why?"

"Because you already live with me," I remind her.

She chuckles as she gets out of the car. "That's only half true. You just never let me go home," she whines.

Ever since that first night she stayed over, I haven't been able to sleep without her.

Maybe that's not healthy.

But I couldn't care less.

She is now my safe haven.

And for someone who has never had that in their life, it's truly something incredibly special, and you never want to lose it once you have it firmly in your grasp.

"My home is your home," I tell her.

"No, this could be my home." She waves her hand to the open house. "I'm buying it, Jake, but..." she pauses and looks back to me, "I do want to live with you. I'm in a good place now. Everything feels great. I like my job, and I love you." She nudges me with her shoulder.

"And the sex is great," I remind her, and she chuckles.

"Yes. Yes, it is," she agrees.

Six months later

. . .

She glances at the ring on her hand, shining it back and forth as we sit in the sun. Her eyes are watering as she looks up at me. How did I manage to fall for the prettiest red head on the planet.

"I didn't need a ring," she says. I reach forward and swipe my finger on her chin wiping away the happy tears she's left there. "Marriage was not the best for me before," she says as she looks back down at her ring. Then she mutters, "But you are also not him, and the way you look at me...." She gazes up at me and in the next instant she is crawling into my lap, where her hands go around my head and she holds onto me. "It's how I've always imagined a husband to look at a wife, the way you look at me. So all the yes's in the world would never suffice, on one condition."

"Name it," I tell her.

"You never stop looking at me like that," she whispers.

I reach up and brush her red locks behind her head.

"I loved you before, and I love you now. Nothing would change that."

"You never know," she says.

I smile at her words.

"Oh, I know. Trust me." She blushes as she stays where she is on my lap, not moving.

"Jake."

"Hmmm." I lean in and kiss the side of her neck.

"I can feel your hard-on." I can't help the smile that touches my lips.

"I can also promise you *that* will never change, *ever*."

"Good." And then I proceed to show her exactly why the way she turns me on will never change, with my mouth, and my cock. As she screams my name. And what a perfect fucking beginning are we.

From now, to the end of time. She will be mine. And not a thing will ever change that.

Thank you for reading A Villain's Kiss. If you enjoyed this book, I would appreciate it if you could leave a review on any platform(s) of your choice.
Reviews are AMAZING for authors, and every one helps!

Kisses,
T.L

Meet Grayson in A Villain's Lies

About the Author

USA Today Best Selling Author T.L. Smith loves to write her characters with flaws so beautiful and dark you can't turn away. Her books have been translated into several languages. If you don't catch up with her in her home state of Queensland, Australia you can usually find her travelling the world, either sitting on a beach in Bali or exploring Alcatraz in San Francisco or walking the streets of New York.

facebook.com/authortlsmith

instagram.com/tlsmith1313

bookbub.com/authors/t-l-smith

tiktok.com/@tlsmith.13

Also by T.L Smith

Sinister Love (Dark Intentions Duet 2)

Cavalier (Crimson Elite #1)

Anguished (Crimson Elite #2)

Conceited (Crimson Elite #3)

Insolent (Crimson Elite #4)

Playette

Love Drunk

Hate Sober

Heartbreak Me (Duet #1)

Heartbreak You (Duet #2)

My Beautiful Poison

My Wicked Heart

My Cruel Lover

Chained Hands

Locked Hearts

Sinful Hands

Shackled Hearts

Reckless Hands

Arranged Hearts

Unlikely Queen

Cruel Queen

Connect with T.L Smith by tlsmithauthor.com

Printed in Great Britain
by Amazon

23473586R00163